The Universe is not required to be in perfect harmony with human ambition

Carl Sagan

FIRST CONTACT

First Contact is a fictional book using imaginary characters or real characters living or dead in fictional situations. Except for the listed acknowledgments, any resemblance to actual persons or their activities is purely coincidental.

Acknowledgments

I wish to thank my friends and either former or current pilots for allowing me to use their names as fictional characters in this book.

Daniel Burns

Thomas Quelly

Kent Fogtman

David Evans

I also want to thank Maggie Trulove, a self-described OCD about grammar person, for proofreading my manuscript. Her comments and improvements are gratefully accepted.

TABLE OF CONTENTS

Preface

Prologue

Chapter 1.

Chapter 2

Chapter 3

Chapter 4

Chapter 5

Chapter 6

Chapter 7

Chapter 8

Chapter 9

Chapter 10

Chapter 11

Chapter 12

Chapter 13

Chapter 14

Chapter 15

Chapter 16

PART TWO – ANDROMEDA

Chapter 17

Chapter 18

Chapter 19

Chapter 20

Chapter 21

Chapter 22

Chapter 23

Chapter 24

Chapter 25

Chapter 26

Chapter 27

Chapter 28

Chapter 29

Chapter 30

Chapter 31

Chapter 32

Chapter 33

Chapter 34

Chapter 35

Chapter 36

Chapter 37

Chapter 38

Chapter 39

Chapter 40

Chapter 41

Epilogue

Afterward

PROLOGUE

The United States chose to remain neutral in World War 1. Following four years of warfare which almost destroyed the European economies, the United States brokered a peace conference. All the warring parties except for Russia attended, as Russia dissolved into civil war, breaking up into multiple nations. The treaty, based on the concept of No Winners, no Losers, returned the national borders, except for Russia's to pre-war levels. The German conquests of the previous Rusian provinces of Poland, Belarus, Estonia. Lithuania and Latvia were affirmed.

In the roaring '20s, J.P. Morgan Jr. arranged for a meeting between Nikola Tesla and Robert Goddard. Tesla, while attempting to develop a better Cupronickel alloy for his alternating current accidentally discovered Cold Fusion in his lab. He successfully demonstrated it to J.P

Morgan, Dr. Coffey, the Chairman of the Science Department at Harvard, and a group of Harvard science professors. Impressed, Morgan sponsored Tesla's research.

Robert Goddard, a pioneer in rocket design, who developed both solid and liquid rocket fuel, successfully tested his rockets. Goddard presented his research to the United States Government, which demonstrated little to no interest. Without stable funding, his research became stymied.

Goddard and Coffey, professional acquaintances, met at a science symposium. Listening to Goddard's frustrations and intrigued by his rocket developments, Coffee arranged a meeting for Goddard with J.P. Morgan. Impressed with Goddard's research, Morgan arranged for Goddard to meet with Tesla. Supervised by Dr. Coffey and his team, Tesla and Goddard successfully tested cold fusion powered rockets at Morgan's Long Island estate. Morgan agreed to bankroll The Goddard and Tesla Rocket Company and purchased land in Roswell, New Mexico, as a test site. Ths space age was born. Within a few years, astronauts, selected from barnstorming airplane pilots orbited the planet.

The United States Government, now profoundly interested, purchased the company and the burgeoning spaceport at Roswell. During the 1940s and '50s, the United States constructed a space station, explored then colonized the moon, and sent an exploratory mission to Mars.

It is true that necessity is the mother of invention. Smaller and higher powered computers became necessary for space flight. The cumbersome punch card computers were first replaced with magnetic tape, then floppy discs, hard discs, and CD drives.

Other nations led by the German Empire, Great Britain, Japan, Italy, France, and the new Russian Federation copied the cold fusion design, and then built their own rockets and orbiting platforms. With the United States controlling the Moon and Mars, during the

1950's the other nations moved on to the asteroid belt and the moons of Jupiter and Saturn to establish their colonies.

Following the establishment of the colonies, independent companies constructed space freighters and moved raw materials, goods, and commodities between the colonial establishments and the orbiting space stations. An active tourist trade developed with many of the independent companies constructing space-borne cruise ships to accommodate this growing market. Domed hotels with facilities deep underground serviced the tourist trade.

With lucrative cargos on trading ships, space piracy developed. The pirates, many secretly sponsored and sheltered by Nikita Kruschev, the Bolshevik governor of the Russian asteroid mining colony, became a menace to shipping. The space-faring nations provided space patrols, but the vastness of space allowed the pirates to flourish.

The pirates intercepted and captured a United

States-flagged luxury cruise ship SS Enchantment. The German Princess Alexandria and her entourage were among the passengers traveling to Mars. Alexandria, the granddaughter of the deceased Kaiser Wilhelm II, cousin to the current Kaiser, and betrothed to the Crown Prince of Austria-Hungary, became the focus of a joint United States Space Patrol and German Empire's Space Navy expedition.

Commodore Robert Treat III commanded the task force which hunted down the pirates and defeated Kruschev's Russian Navy. The space battle and the near-destruction of one of the German naval cruisers ignited a war between the Russian Federation and the German Empire, which threatened to draw in all of Europe.

Tri-party negotiations initiated by the United States averted a full-scale war. The capture of Kruschev and the rescue of Princess Alexandria ended the crisis. Receiving the Russian asteroid colony as reparations, the Germans lifted the siege of St Petersburg, and their army returned to Germany.

The humiliated Russian Federation dissolved into civil war. Yuri Andropov, the head of state security and a secret Bolshevik, revolted splintering Russia and took control of Russia east of the Urals. Andrei Gromyko, the Foreign Minister, and leader of the Socialists, consolidated power in European Russia. The factions fought over and ultimately destroyed the Russian Space Station, with most of the debris falling on Russia or in the Pacific Ocean.

The Far Eastern Republic declared its independence and allied with the Japanese Empire and Mongolia. Kazakhstan and Ukraine also became independent nations and drove the warring factions out of their territory.

Commodore Treat, promoted to Admiral, became the military governor of Mars. Two of his patrolling frigates intercepted and destroyed two of three pirate warships attacking a tourist liner. Fire from the frigates disabled and holed the escaping pirate. Determined to capture the derelict pirate vessel, on a ballistic path into outer space, one of the frigates chased after the potential prize until it was drawn into an anomaly in the area. Suddenly an opening appeared shining like a bright light. The pirate vessel was pulled into the portal and disappeared.

Repetitive surveys across the opening indicated it was a tunnel. The frigates documented the location and characteristics of the anomaly and wirelessed Admiral Treat. Several days later, Treat, aboard his flagship, the dreadnaught USSP Washington, and a flotilla of support warships arrived.

Drones, programmed to return, flew into the gateway and back. Readings demonstrated that humans could safely make the passage. Treat sent one frigate through, and when it returned led the flotilla into the portal. Upon arriving at the other side, scanners identified the star system to be Delta Pavonis, twenty light years from Earth. Interstellar travel became a possibility.

Explorations found a habitable planet and several other portals. Traveling through the gateways, the explorers discovered other star systems and portals. Within fifteen years, the space-faring nations detected habitable planets on star systems within thirty light-years of Sol and established colonies.

One of the worlds, orbiting Beta Hydri, contained evidence of a destroyed civilization tens of thousands of years old. Following several years of careful excavations, the researchers discovered a time capsule amongst the ruins. When opened it held hard discs. Following several months of effort, a translation developed.

A very human-like species warred with an upright feline-like species called the Krieg. Both used nuclear weapons to destroy each other. The last discs indicated that the human survivors evacuated the planet. The researchers did not discover the location of the Krieg world. The cold reality set in. We are not alone!!

Recalled to Washington, Vice Admiral Treat, and his science adviser Dr. DePietro testified before joint House and Senate committees to give first-hand accounts of the discoveries on Beta Hydri 4. Humanity now knew the identity of a potential enemy. What was unknown was how many other intelligent species existed, and were they dangerous.

DiPietro provided scientific testimony about the nuclear war between the human inhabitants of Beta Hydri 4 and the Krieg. During the approximate thirty-thousand years since the war, the residual radiation decayed enough to make the planet habitable again. He also theorized that other gateways, with currently unknown identification markers, were likely to present passageways to the Krieg homeworld, and the escape paths for the departing humans. He postulated the importance of discovering those gateways and of any which led to Earth.

Treat focused his testimony on the means to protect Earth and her colonial planets. He urged the politicians to set aside nationalistic goals to focus on the survival of the human race. He reiterated former President Rockefeller's idea of a united planetary defense force. He postulated the need for orbital defense platforms around Earth, the colonial worlds and system-wide protection for the gateways.

President Reagan than assigned Treat to attend an international conference attended by all the space-faring nations. The purpose was to establish the groundwork for military cooperation among the countries.

Chapter 1

March 1, 1978. Washington DC

Following the international conference, President Reagan invited Vice Admiral Treat and Emily to the White House. In a Rose Garden Ceremony, Reagan promoted Treat to a Four-Star Admiral and appointed him as *Chief of Naval Operations*. The Senate quickly confirmed the appointment. Admiral Treat and Emily moved into their official residence at Number One Observatory Circle, at the United States Naval Observatory in Washington DC.

As CNO, Treat reported directly to the Secretary of the Navy and became a member of the Joint Chiefs of Staff. He also became an advisor to President Reagan and worked with Congress to secure appropriations for warships and defense platforms. Treat also headed the task force working with the other space powers for mutual defense.

Reagan gave Rear Admiral Alan Shepard his third star with the promotion to Vice Admiral. Shepard replaced Treat as Tactical Commander of the United States Space Patrol. Shephard now commanded seventy-five warships, including seven new dreadnaughts, all larger and faster than *USSP Washington* class.

The new *Michigan Class* increased size and tonnage by fifty percent. Technical improvements in miniaturized computers and hard drives generating Gigabytes of memory controlled the fusion reactors and increased the speed of the vessels to .01C (lightspeed) or 6,700,000 miles per hour. The upgraded computerized powerplants doubled the warships' destructive power of the laser batteries. The larger size of the dreadnaughts increased by one-half the number of missiles and launchers. Doubling the size of the launch and retrieval bays increased the number of warbirds to ninety per vessel.

Treat planned to repurpose the older

dreadnaughts of the *USSP Washington Class* to the defense of the gateways. Treat's proposed re-design included removing the long-range missiles and replacing them with railguns shooting large chunks of metal or rocks.

Stationing the older dreadnaughts as support vessels to patrol adjacent to the gateways would allow them to fire objects with great kinetic force at an emerging enemy. Combined with enhanced laser batteries, the railguns should provide the defenders with sufficient time to inflict considerable damage on an invading fleet within the sixty to ninety-second computer blackout after the invaders transited the gateway.

In his capacity of CNO, Treat was invited by President Reagan to sit in at cabinet meetings. Working closely with the Secretary of Defense, Casper Weinberger, Treat assisted in the development of the concept to construct the orbital defense platforms. Treat testified before Congress about the proposals, and he provided details on various plans for the defense platforms with cost estimates. President Reagan proposed a ten percent increase in defense spending. The debate dragged on into the summer. Most in Congress demanded the rest of the world's nations participate in shouldering the costs.

President Reagan proposed to convene a conference of the space-faring nations at Breton Woods, NH, to jointly develop the platforms to a standard design and defense structure. Once accepted, a design could also be used at the colonial planets. The asteroids in each system were excellent sources of the raw materials needed for construction.

Chapter 2

October 1, 1978 – Breton Woods.

Secretary of Defense Casper Weinberger and Admiral Robert Treat welcomed the delegates to the conference. The first guests to arrive were the delegations from Germany and Austria-Hungary. Attendees included Hans Apel, the German Defense Minister, Admiral Scheer, and the Austro-Hungarian Prime Minister Kurt Waldheim.

The next delegation included The United Kingdom, represented by the Secretary of Defense for State, Francis Pym, and the First Sea Lord Sir Henry Leach. The newly elected Prime Minister Margaret Thatcher attended the opening ceremonies, then visited with President Reagan in Washington DC.

Japan arrived next, led by Crown Prince Akihito, the Commander in Chief of the military, and the Prime Minister, Takeo Fukuda. Akihito previously rejected a joint command structure but was open to a standardized defense platform.

The joint Italian-French delegation arrived. Previously those two countries combined their space efforts as the expenses of competing with the other nations strained their economies. The French Defense Minister. Raymond Barre, and the Italian Foreign Minister, Franco Malfatti, headed that delegation.

Reagan invited Liberia, as she was the largest state sponsor of mercantile activities in space. Close to fifty percent of the merchant and cruiseliner vessels were Liberian flagged. The Foreign Secretary, Elisha Taylor, the great-grandson of the former President, and the Secretary of Defense, Alonzo Driver, great-grandson of the famous general, headed the Liberian delegation. Liberia leased extensive tracts of the Moon and Mars as bases of operation. Liberia, which boasted of the sixth largest space patrol fleet, also had space stations above Mars and the Moon as transit, shipbuilding, and repair facilities.

Other attending nations included Greece, a partner in the German and Austro-Hungarian space program, and Australia, a partner in the UK program. India and Brazil, which were new entries in space travel, also sent delegations. Both nations recently finished constructing their first orbiting space stations.

Following an evening reception, including the delegations and their spouses, President Reagan opened the conference with an address he titled *A Time for Choosing*. In his 30-minute speech, he highlighted several salient points.

 - We are now potentially facing the most dangerous enemy to the human race. There can not be any peace without preparation for war.

 - If we lose, there is no place to escape.

 - Those of us who have the most to lose, are doing the least to prevent a holocaust.

- Many are advocating doing nothing, as the Krieg warriors have not made an appearance in thirty-thousand years. We don't know that, as up to a few hundred years ago, humanity was a barbarous lot without industrialization or even radio waves to announce our presence. Now we have made ourselves known in interstellar space.

 - Humanity's age-old dream of space colonization and even existence in itself is in danger of extinction. Divided, we could cease to exist. Together we can fulfill our dreams.

The gathering received the President's speech with resounding applause. He thanked them all and expressed confidence in their deliberations. Upon his departure, a helicopter brought him to Pease Air Force Base in Portsmouth, where he boarded Air Force One for his flight back to Washington, DC, to attend his private meeting with Margaret Thatcher. The spouses adjourned to a separate reception, and the delegates to a large meeting room, seated at tables set up for the national delegations.

Vice-President Gerald Ford gaveled the meeting to order and presented the prearranged agenda. In his opening remarks, he suggested the individual delegations be divided into committees of the whole. Each multi-national committee would handle an agenda item then bring it back to the entire commission for revisions and/or a vote.

The multi-national composition of the committees prevented the national interests of one or more nations from derailing the conference. It also assigned responsibility and accountability to the committees. Realizing the simplicity and effectiveness of that plan, Greece made a motion to accept the proposal, and Brazil seconded. Following a brief discussion, it was unanimously approved.

Following two weeks of meetings and debates, a pentagon-shaped design gained approval. The plan included the sides of the stations to bristle with heavy laser batteries, with retractable long-range missile battery launchers and rail-guns located top and bottom. Internal hangers would contain up to one-hundred warbirds capable of launch from four directions simultaneously. Electronic domes and transmitters could be situated both topside and underside. A gravitational spin would provide eighty percent Earth-normal gravity.

Each of the existing space powers agreed to construct two of the defense platforms to defend Earth. Australia, Greece, Brazil, and India each decided to build one. Liberia consented to erect a platform to assist in defense of the Moon, and another for the protection of Mars.

Prevalent nationalism eliminated the potential for an international defense force. The nations did decide upon a mutual defense pact, the sharing of intelligence, and to hold quarterly meetings. Each power would be responsible for constructing defenses at their colonial planets.

After the conference, President Reagan

requested the Joint Chiefs of Staff meet to better allocate United States military personnel. The JCS decided that army personnel would command and staff the orbital defenses above Earth, and the ground and orbital defenses of the colonial worlds.

Navy personnel would defend the gateways and be crew members of the United States Space Patrol. The Air Force would provide pilots for the warbirds at the defense platforms protecting Earth, the Moon, and Mars. However, in grade transfers of qualified pilots between the services were permitted as the pilots all flew the same Joint Strike Fighter.

Chapter 3

September 5, 1980.

Beta Hydri

The cruiser *USSP Indianapolis*, escorted by the frigate *USS Kearsarge* and the destroyer *USSP Simmons*, conducted a routine patrol of the Ort Cloud at the extremes of the system. The helmsman of *Simmons* notified Lt. Commander Kenneth Mattingly of an unknown type of disturbance in space twenty-thousand miles ahead. Mattingly ordered the dispatch of a probe to observe the anomaly and sent a wireless to Captain John Young aboard *Indianapolis*. Young ordered Mattingly to hold his position until *Kearsarge* and *Indianapolis* arrived.

One hour later, as Commander Edgar Mitchell, skipper of *Kearsarge,* arrived on station, a gateway appeared, and a small object moving at .25 of lightspeed emerged, emitting a high-resolution broadband scan directed towards the star. Mattingly instructed their robot to scan the gate and the intruder then transmit all the compiled data back to *Simmons*.   Once he analyzed the data, Mattingly transferred it to Young and Mitchell.

Upon arrival, Captain Young ordered a video-conference with Mitchell and Mattingly. The data clearly demonstrated an unknown gateway and an unmanned device traveling at high speed. The characteristics of the anomaly were very different from those of previously discovered gateways. Young wirelessed Beta Hydri 4 that an unknown intruder was inbound. The base commander, Captain Eugene Cernan, placed the system on high alert and wirelessed the gateway probe to transit to Delta Pavonis 4 and inform Admiral Shepard.

Receiving the wireless message from the probe, Vice Admiral Shepard placed Armstrong Base on Delta Pavonis 4 on alert and signaled the robot at the gateway to Sol System to transit and warn Earth that an intruder device was inbound to Beta Hydri 4.

While waiting for instructions, Shephard ordered Rear Admiral of the lower half, Neil Armstrong, on the Michigan Class dreadnaught *USSP Wisconsin*, and his task force to transit to Beta Hydri. *Wisconsin's* escorts included three cruisers, *USSP Baltimore, USSP Boston, USSP Nashville*, and the frigates, USSP *Bromstein*, USSP *McCloy*, USSP *Garcia*, USSP *Bradley*, USSP *McDonnell*, USSP *Brumby*, and *USSP Davidson*. The estimated time to transit was two days.

Having received regular updates, Armstrong ordered the intruder not to be intercepted or disturbed. He ordered Captain Young to send a robot to follow if the intruder exited from the same spot.

The probe flew past Beta Hydri 4 at a distance of one-hundred-thousand miles, scanning the planet as it passed. It then slingshotted around the star, studying it again while on course to return to the portal. Young positioned *Indianapolis* near the gateway coordinates as the intruder zoomed past. Young then dispatched two probes into the entrance, with one to scan the new system with return coordinates, the other to follow the visitor.

Two hours later, the first probe came back. Initial scans indicated a binary star system without planets in the habitable zone. An analysis of star charts predicted the system to be Mu Cassiopeiae, approximately five and one-half light years from Eta Cassiopeiae and almost twenty-five light years from Sol.

The second probe continued the chase of the alien in an attempt to determine its course. The alien device soon outdistanced its pursuer and disappeared off the scanners. One day later, the probe with its data reentered the gateway back into the Delta Pavonis system.

Luna City

As part of his CNO duties, Admiral Treat visited the defense networks on the moon. Following the discovery of large quantities of ice buried under the polar regions, Luna City became the most significant metropolis not situated on Earth. Underground aqueducts supplied the domed city with fresh water and oxygen. Recycling was mandatory, with oxygen scrubbers removing the carbon from CO_2, and all waste products were reprocessed. Those measures allowed over two-hundred-thousand residents to inhabit the city, which also extended twelve levels underground. Luna City also provided shore leave for the many uniformed and civilian personnel living and working on the orbiting facilities, as well as a vibrant tourist industry.

The space patrol maintained five hardened installations beneath the surface. These contained shuttle terminals, with underground subways leading between the facilities, and to Luna City. Marines provided routine patrols and defensive capabilities including missiles, e-laser turrets, and anti-missile defense batteries. The Marines also protected the orbiting space docks and shipbuilding facilities with similar equipment.

The Admiral was beginning his tour of the recently completed United States defense platform when the notification of the visitor intrusion arrived from Admiral Shepard. Treat immediately shuttled down to the Naval Command Center at Luna City where he obtained Shepard's official report. After reviewing the report, Treat sent it with his recommendations back to Washington, DC. He then dined at the Officers Club, where he received instructions from Weinberger to return to Earth.

The next day, following Treat's recommendations, Admiral Armstrong's fleet transited into Beta Hydri and took up station at Beta Hydri 4. Armstrong ordered *Indianapolis, Simmons,* and *Kearsarge* to enter the gateway and use the new data to search for additional alien portals.

Armstrong invited all the ship commanders to shuttle over to *USSP Wisconsin* for a conference. His Flag Lieutenant Jonathan Bascomb greeted the arriving officers and escorted them to the admiral's ready room. Flag Captain Robert Crippen met them there, and stewards provided refreshments while waiting for the Admiral. Bascomb waited outside the room and loudly announced:

"Admiral on Deck" when Armstrong strode into the room. The officers all jumped to attention until Armstrong reached the podium.

Crippen then stated: "Gentlemen, be seated." The gathered officers quietly found their seats while Lieutenant Bascomb hung a three-dimensional star chart from the ceiling. Once installed he stepped aside. Then the Admiral strode to the podium and began:

"Gentlemen, I called you here together so that you can meet and greet one another to facilitate a cohesive group. Vice Admiral Shepard cobbled together this task force from available ships. Captain Crippen is the senior captain and is designated my second in command.

As you are all aware, we have been visited and scanned by another space-faring race. We do not know the intruders' intentions, or even who they are. The visitors could be the Kreig, the humans who escaped this planet, or someone or something else. However, we must be prepared for an anticipated visit as our presence here is now known.

Could the future be war or peace? We don't know, but what is entirely likely is that it probably will begin here. As of today, our readiness status is DEFCON 3. The news has undoubtedly reached Earth. Until we receive new instructions or assistance, we are the first line of defense.

Currently, one defense platform is in service and the second should be completed within a month. I recalled Captain John Young's task force. He left drones to monitor the new gateway with programming to report any activity and transits. The robots then will shadow any intruders. Captain Crippen will post your patrol assignments tomorrow. Shore leaves are permitted, although two full shifts must be available for duty at all times. All personnel on shore leave must wear their communication units at all times. Enjoy your stay at the station, get some chow, then return to your ships. Your orders will be posted on your personal computers. Dismissed."

After the Admiral left the room, the officers milled about discussing the situation in private conversations. Most of the Space Patrol officers and crews had never seen any hostile action. If war came, it would be their baptism of fire.

Within two months, Captain Young and his flotilla discovered two additional portals leading into red dwarf star systems with no habitable zone planets. Young then gathered his ships, positioned drones at the gateways, and returned to Beta Hydri 4. There he reported his findings to Admiral Armstrong. During the meeting, Armstrong advised him of his pending promotion to Rear Admiral of the Lower Half and gave him new orders to return to Earth.

Chapter 4

Washington, DC

The headlines in newspapers pronounced in bold letters: **THE ALIENS ARE HERE.** The news columns below were partially factual, but mostly wild speculation. The shocked stock market lost ten percent of its value in one day, before stabilizing at a twelve percent loss after a week of wild fluctuations.

Television news broadcasts attempted a more balanced view, as the news anchors' jobs required them to stand up and present the news. They were the face of the networks. Soberly, NBC's John Chancellor, CBS's Dan Rather, and ABC's Peter Jennings tried to sort fact from fiction, conducting interviews with politicians and retired military officers. On a Sunday evening following the breaking news, 60-Minutes devoted the whole hour to the topic.

President Reagan held a news conference. In a very composed voice, he attempted to reassure the country that his administration was working to evaluate all the information available. They were consulting with the other space powers to determine a course of action. All reserve military forces were directed to report to their units within forty-eight hours. However, at this time, there was no imminent threat.

Reagan called a Cabinet meeting in the situation room with Vice President Ford attending. Other principal attendees included Secretary of State Alexander Haig, Secretary of Defense Weinberger, Secretary of the Navy John Lehman, The Secretary of the Army, John Marsh, The Secretary of the Interior, James B. Watt, and the CIA Director, William Casey. The Secretaries of the Navy and the Army directly reported to the Secretary of Defense. The purpose was to assess the threat and determine international support. Reagan spoke first:

"Gentlemen, we all knew contact with an

advanced alien species was not only possible but highly likely. That likelihood is now a reality. Some people draw encouragement that the visitors used passive scans, and are likely friendly. I don't share that viewpoint. The first contact between European explorers and the Caribbean native tribes was also peaceful. The Europeans returned as Conquistadors. We must be prepared nationally and internationally to confront the potential threat. The United States, as the preeminent world power, must take the lead, both diplomatically and militarily."

Looking at Alexander Haig, Reagan asked, "What is your information on the diplomatic front?"

Haig replied, "Mr. President, I just returned from a conference call with our European Allies. The meeting included the German Chancellor, Helmut Schmidt, the Foreign Minister, Hans-Dietrich Genscher, the Defense Minister, Hans Apel, Kurt Waldheim, the Prime Minister of Austria-Hungary, and Maggie Thatcher and Sir

Francis Pym from the UK. They all have agreed to comply with the Breton Woods mutual defense agreement. Their navies are on alert and will respond as needed.

"The Liberians are also honoring the agreement. Most of their fleet is comprised of fast frigates and cruisers and will be a valuable addition. Their Secretary of Defense, Alonzo Driver, is a retired ship's captain with experience in convoy protection. He was reactivated to be commodore of their fleet. Their engineers are close to finishing their assigned defense platforms above Luna City and Marsopolis. The Liberian military will staff and defend those stations.

"Other space-faring nations are waiting for developments. The French, Italians, and Greeks will also participate in the event of an attack. In the meantime, they continue to work on completing their defense platforms.

"Japan is non-committal. Crown Prince Akihito indicated he will assess the threat if it develops.

The Far Eastern Republic, never a meaningful player in space, will likely follow Japan's lead. I suspect they could soon be absorbed into Japan's Co-prosperity Sphere. Currently, they are economically and militarily dependent on Japan.

"Brazil and Australia are constructing their assigned defense platforms. However, both are behind schedule due to cost overruns. Neither country will be able to provide meaningful help beyond finishing what they started.

"Gromyko's Russian Republic has allied with Kazakhstan to re-enter space. The Kazak's rebuilt their launch center, which was destroyed in the civil wars. Combined with the Russians, they are launching vessels and placing materials in orbit for a new space station. Nothing more can be expected of them at this time.

"Soviet Russia is utilizing newly discovered substantial deposits of coal, oil, and natural gas to rebuild and re-energize their power grid.

Most of Soviet Russia is still dark at night. If they survive long enough, It will take years, maybe decades, for them to catch up with the rest of the world's economies.

"The quarterly meeting of the space-faring nations is scheduled for Geneva in two weeks. We could have a better understanding of their preparations before that meeting."

Reagan thanked Haig for his summary, then urged him to keep up the pressure. Reagan then looked at Secretary of Defense Casper.

After looking at Marsh and Lehman, who were seated on either side of him, Weinberger began, "I provided all of you with copies of reports compiled by Secretaries John Marsh and John Lehman. Those reports provided details of our deployments. I will summarize. The Moon defense platform is complete and is being staffed. Simulations are being conducted, and the weapons testing is in process. The four warbird squadrons are en route and are running practice operations during the flight. The expectations are for full operational status within a week. Once there they will conduct additional simulated combat training with the five Moon based squadrons, which are found in hardened launch facilities. The pilots will swap out defender and aggressor roles.

"Both of the platforms defending our space-borne assets above Earth are operational. They provide offensive and defensive firepower to protect the space above North America. The geosynchronous orbits will extend that protection through Central America, but will not be useful much below Columbia. There are five squadrons of fighters at each station, backed up by one-hundred squadrons based throughout the United States. The Brazilians need to expedite the construction of their defense platform. Without it, South America will be unprotected.

"The two defense platforms above Mars are operational. One protects the orbiting space station and the other the military shipyard. The Liberian platform defends their commercial and military docks and shipyards. Mars Base

Command will coordinate activities at all of the spaceborne facilities. Alonzo Driver has promised total cooperation.

"Defense platforms are in the final stages of construction at the colonial worlds. Delta Pavonis 4 will have two, with one currently operational, and the others will have one each. These facilities are constructed from planetary raw materials and those found at the system's asteroids. The new workers, engineers, and military garrisons have doubled the colony's populations. Hardened shelters are available to house the colonists in an emergency. Given the unknown nature of the potential threat, we are prepared as well as can be."

Reagan thanked Weinberger, then addressed CIA Director George H W Bush, asking, "Director, what is your assessment?"

Bush responded, "Mr. President, we have agents and assets working throughout the world. Other assets are at the various international space colonies to get a feel of the preparations and the mood of the colonists. I have shared that intelligence with Alexander and Casper, and they have included it in their analysis.

"Information from the Japanese colonies is sketchy. Their government carefully screens all applicants. Foreign travelers are viewed with suspicion and continuously followed. It would appear that Prince Akihito takes the threat seriously and has deployed two dreadnaught class battleships, the *IJN Nagato* and her sister ship *IJN Matsu,* plus support vessels, to Sigma Draconis.

"There is no definitive information about their planetary defense preparations or military deployments. We did provide their government with the characteristics of the intruder's gateway. I suspect their naval forces are actively searching."

Reagan then asked the Secretary of the Interior for his analysis.

Watt began, "Mr. President, your speech yesterday seems to have calmed the American population. They have not dealt with an external threat for over a century. When the news of the alien probe broke, rioting and civil disturbances broke out in several lower-income urban neighborhoods with widespread looting. The local police, caught by surprise, needed help from State Police and National Guard units. The rioting diminished after three days, particularly after the arrest of many of the leaders. Curfews are still in effect in the riot-torn neighborhoods, and police are conducting sweeps to round up any of the escaped leadership.

"During last weeks governors' conference, I stressed the need for regional police cooperation. The governors agreed, but many of their computer systems do not effectively communicate with each other. There are teams of IT engineers working to resolve the interface problems. It is a doable goal, which just needs time to address.

"The population at large is on edge, but your speech and news conference seems to be lowering tensions. Numerous patriotic rallies are scheduled for this weekend, which is the first Saturday for college football. The hamburgers, hot dogs, and flag-waving are sure to boost the public's spirits.

"All in all, I like the general trend of the mood of the country. What we need is a return to normalcy with the government going about its daily activities. The news agencies can be provided with periodic updates on our preparations, all of it encapsulated in everyday business. Our answers to questions need to be open and transparent while working to change the focus of attention."

Reagan thanked them all for their input and adjourned the meeting, setting the next scheduled cabinet meeting for the following week.

Chapter 5

The Presidential elections were in full swing. After serving three terms, Ronald Reagan decided to retire with Nancy to Rancho del Cielo in the Santa Ynez Mountains northwest of Santa Barbara, California. The election projected to be spirited and included the candidates from the three major parties.

The Fusion Party nomination battle initially was wide open with six candidates, Vice President Gerald Ford, CIA Director George H. W. Bush, Representative John Anderson, the Fusion Party House Conference Chairperson and number three in the party's hierarchy in the House, Howard Baker, Senator from Tennessee, Lowell Weicker, Senator from Connecticut, and Robert Dole, Senator from Kansas.

The early primaries weeded out Dole, Weicker, and Baker. The last six primary elections see-sawed between Ford and Bush, with Anderson, consistently lagging behind. California finally provided Ford with over fifty-five percent of the delegates. Bush withdrew and endorsed Ford, who subsequently named him as his running mate.

Anderson, disgruntled with the Ford/Bush deal, decided to run as an independent. He previously hoped for an alliance with Bush to add planks to the party's platform. Anderson selected Patrick Lucey, former Governor of Wisconsin, as his running mate.

The Republicans waged a three-way fight between former Texas Governor John Connally, Representative Philip Crane from Illinois, and Senator Larry Pressler from South Dakota. Connally easily won the nomination on the first ballot. He then chose Phil Crane for Vice President, hoping for the Illinois electoral votes.

The Democrat-Socialists renamed their party the Social Democrats after the debacle in 1968. Their candidates included Senator Walter Mondale from Minnesota, Frank Church from Idaho, John Kennedy from Massachusetts,

Jimmy Carter, Governor of Georgia, and Clifford Finch, retiring Governor of Mississippi.

Jimmy Carter won the Iowa Caucuses, and Kennedy won the New Hampshire Primary the following week. Jimmy Carter won in South Carolina, and he and Finch split the Super Tuesday vote among Georgia, Florida, Mississippi, Alabama, Tennessee, and Arkansas. Several other primaries were indecisive with delegates divided among the candidates.

Sensing voter dissatisfaction with the candidates, Jerry Brown, Senator from California entered the fray. He won the primaries in Maryland, New Jersey, Rhode Island, Oregon, and California. He began the Convention in New York in third place behind Carter and Finch.

The first ballot ended up Carter, Kennedy, Brown, Finch, Mondale, and Church. On the fifth ballot, Brown took the lead, with Kennedy in second place. On the seventh ballot, Finch threw his support to Brown, leaving him seventy-five votes from victory. Mondale and Church withdrew before the eighth ballot, freeing their delegates who spread their votes between Brown, Carter, and Kennedy. Brown finally won a bare majority on the tenth ballot.

The next day he chose Finch as his running mate. Brown earned a hard-fought nomination which turned into a Phyrric Victory. Following the Finch deal, the convention exploded with loud condemnations and a walkout of the Kennedy and Carter delegates.

On November 4, 1980, the Fusion Party ticket of Ford/Bush won forty-eight percent of the vote, The Republicans won thirty percent, the Social-Democrats won sixteen percent, and Anderson/Lucey won six percent. The Fusionists gained five senators and ten house seats, mostly from the Social-Democrats who lost four in the Senate and eight in the House.

One week after the election, the Social-Democrat Central Committee called for a meeting to plot the future of the party.

Attendees included Senators Brown, Kennedy, Mondale, Church, Governor Carter, and Finch. After two disastrous presidential elections, the party was in danger of sinking into irrelevance. After three days of finger-pointing, the party was no closer to agreement than before the meeting began. They finally agreed to meet again in January.

Frustrated by their declining political prospects, radical elements of the party embraced anarchy and began terrorist actions against government buildings. On December 1, 1980, bomb explosions occurred at the Capitol Building and the Pentagon, causing thousands of dollars in damage, but fortunately, no one was killed. On the same day, police discovered and defused a more massive bomb inside the Washington Monument.

The FBI investigation revealed that two staff members of Social-Democrat Senator Harvey Stein of Washington, Kathleen Smith, and Rolando Duvalle, were present in both the Capitol Building and Pentagon on December 1.

Security cameras indicated they were also on the grounds of the Washington Monument.

Obtaining search warrants, the FBI raided their apartments and discovered bomb-making materials similar to the defused bomb. Arrest warrants were issued. Informed of the raids, the terrorists attempted to escape, driving in Kathleen's car to Miami. Both were removed from a Pan-American flight to Brazil at the Miami International Airport and taken into custody. Senator Stein condemned the attacks and denied any knowledge or involvement. A subsequent investigation by both the Senate and the FBI cleared his name.

In response, President Reagan created a new cabinet post, the Department of Homeland Security which consolidated various law enforcement operations in one department. The primary responsibilities included anti-terrorism, border security, immigration, customs, disaster prevention and management, and electronic cyber-security. The latter was deemed very important as the fusion power reactors were interconnected in regional grids.

President-elect Gerald Ford consulted with Reagan on who should be appointed to head the new department. Vice Admiral Robert Treat, the current CNO was the top choice. The Treats attended the White House Christmas Party. There the President and President-elect took them aside and made the offer. Robert looked at Emily who smiled broadly, then accepted. Two days later, he submitted the resignation of his commission to the Secretary of the Navy, John Lehman, effective January 1, 1981. Two weeks later the Senate confirmed him as the first Secretary of Homeland Security.

Chapter 6

On Tuesday, January 20, 1981, Chief Justice Warren Burger administered the oath of office as President of the United States to Gerald Ford. Minutes later, Associate Justice Potter Stuart administered the oath of office as Vice President to George H.W. Bush. Two rows back, Robert and Emily Treat looked on as witnesses. Subsequently, Ronald and Nancy Reagan boarded Air Force 1 for the flight to Los Angelas and a motorcade to Rancho del Cielo and retirement.

On Thursday, January 22, President Ford called a meeting of his crucial advisors in the Oval Office. Attendees included Vice President Bush, Secretary of State George Schultz, Attorney General Edwin Meese, Secretary of Defense Donald Rumsfeld, and Secretary of Homeland Security Robert Treat.

Ford began, "Gentlemen, I provided you notes taken from President Reagan's September meeting on the Beta Hydri issue. Since that time, the second defense platform at Delta Pavonis 4 was completed. Additionally, the platforms at Eta Cassiopeiae A and B and Alpha Centauri are operational. A new installation is under construction above Beta Hydri 4 to defend the planet and space dock."

Looking at the Attorney, General Ford stated, "Ed, I need for you to prepare martial law options for the inhabited colony worlds, and the asteroid mining consortiums. In the event of an attack, plans need to be in place to immediately take whatever measures are legally deemed necessary to protect those worlds. The actions must not be open to criticism of a government power grab."

Addressing the Secretary of State, Ford stated, "George, please provide me with a detailed report of activities of foreign nations since the September meeting. I am particularly interested in Brazil's and Australia's progress on their defense platforms. Brazil will be covering our southern flank, and Australia needs to step up to assist in defense of the southern hemisphere. Also, try to obtain all the intelligence available on the Japanese preparations. They attend the quarterly meetings, but other than assurances, they have not been forthcoming with specifics."

Speaking to the Secretary of Defense, Ford opined, "Donald, consult with the Joint Chiefs to determine their readiness of defenses in orbit and on the moon. I want a down and dirty analysis of the actual situation, and contingency planning. I don't want a wish list, just priorities."

Looking at the Secretary of Homeland Security, Ford said, "You all know our newest Secretary, Robert Treat. Robert and Emily will leave next week on a tour of the colonial worlds. Robert will use his experience and influence as the prior Commander of Spaceborne forces to evaluate the readiness of the orbiting and ground-based defense facilities.

"Emily has accepted the new position of Deputy

Secretary of Defense for Colonial Administration and will report directly to the Secretary. She will access the coordination between the military governors and military police with civilian officials, and locally elected sheriffs.

"Emily will also evaluate the extent of training at the dragon facility. Up to now, officials are using the domesticated dragons for aerial surveys and search and rescue operations. However, equipped with cameras, the reptiles could additionally have military reconnaissance capabilities in the guise of natural events. We can also conduct experiments to determine if the dragons can be relocated to other planets without disrupting the local ecosystems. All of Emily's recommendations will be brought to Rumsfeld's attention."

Ford ended the meeting stating, "We will meet again in April. I anticipate full progress reports from all of you."

Chapter 7

On Monday, January 29, Robert and Emily boarded a shuttle to the Apollo Space Station, where the Michigan Class super dreadnaught *USSP Enterprise* waited with Task Force One to take them on their journey to the colonies. Before embarking, they accepted the video invitation of the station commander, General Gus Grissom, to tour the massive facility and to dine with him at his table in the Officers' Club.

Grissom's aide, Lieutenant John Connolly met Robert and Emily as they debarked the shuttle. He assigned their luggage for transport to *USSP Enterprise,* then escorted them to a tram for the tour of Apollo Station, including the impressive array of defense systems. The naval officer in Robert closely examined the laser and missile batteries. He took notes of the positioning of the emplacements and viewed simulations depicting the defense against a hostile attack. Two hours later, the tram driver stopped at the Officers' Club, and Lt. Connolly brought them to

General Grissim's table.

Seeing them approach, General Grissom and two naval officers stood up. Grissom said: "Thank you, Mr. Connolly. You are dismissed."

Then addressing Robert, he stated: "Mr. Secretary, you already know Rear Admiral of the Lower Half, John Young, and his Flag Captain, Robert Crippen. Please introduce us to your lovely and famous wife."

Emily blushed slightly and then produced a radiant smile as Robert introduced her. Following Robert's introductions, Emily stated, "I don't know about famous, but as long as you don't refer to me as the *Dragon Lady,* I am good." The ice was broken, and general laughter ensued. Then as the servers approached, everyone sat down.

Robert briefed Grissom, Young, and Crippin on the scope of his mission. He stressed that he was operating under the President's authority and that his and Emily's trip was not a political junket. President Ford wanted a detailed report before April.

Emily enchanted the officers with the retelling of her adventures including the domestication of wild animals, organizing hunts, and the taming and training of the dragons. The officers afforded her rapt attention as she described herself saddling and riding the dragons. Emily expressed the exhilaration of flight and emphasized that the dragon and rider worked as a team based on trust and reliance. She made the analogy to a cavalryman and his horse.

General Grissom asked, "I have heard of many instances of riders falling off a horse. How do you prevent falls off the dragon while in flight?"

Emily replied." The rider wears a full body safety harness which clips onto the stirrups and both sides of the saddle. An attendant will adjust the harness straps to fit the rider. "That adjustment allows the pilot room to shift in the seat but not fall out. I also wear a flight helmet, with UV tinted face shield, and built-in wireless communication."

Admiral Young asked, "Have you ever hunted while riding the dragons"?

Emily replied, "Several times, I used my repeating crossbow. There is no sport in using a blaster." I developed a scabbard to hold the weapon."

Young asked, "How do you control the direction of the dragon's flight if your hands are busy with the crossbow"?

Emily replied, "With my knees pushing into the animal's body on either side, tap or push with my left for a right turn, and with my right for leftward direction. Once the rider works with the animal, they develop rapport and become as one."

Captain Crippin asked, "Do you foresee military usages of the dragons"?

Emily replied, "With proper training, dragon and rider teams could be used for observation, search and rescue, and even stealth sniper teams using the crossbow. I am sure you military-minded fellows can be really creative. My job was to demonstrate that it could be done. It is up to you to realize the potential."

Admiral Young looked at the clock and stated, "We depart for Delta Pavonis in three hours. We need to get back to *Enterprise* and prepare."

With that, Grissom signaled for the waiter, signed the check, and everyone prepared to leave.

Chapter 8

At the stroke of midnight, January 30, 1981, the Harbormaster released the docking clamps connecting *USSP Enterprise* to Berth A at the Naval Space Dock. Helmsman Lt. Jeffrey Smith used thrusters to move *Enterprise* free of the dock, and space tugs reorientated her for departure.

Captain Crippin then gave the order "Mr. Smith, take us out to join the fleet."

Slowly, then gradually gaining speed, *USSP Enterprise* headed towards her consorts.

Twenty miles out, the heavy cruisers *USSP Augusta* and *USSP Concord* waited with the frigates *USSP Hepburn, USSP Connole, USSP Rathburn, USSP Lang, USSP Reasoner, USSP Bagley,* two passenger liners, two troop ships and three cargo ships for *Enterprise* to join them. When *Enterprise* arrived on station, the escorts fanned out into an inverted "V" formation with the cruisers on point, the frigates on either wing and *Enterprise* in the middle followed by the troop and cargo ships.

The liner and the two troop ships were converted cruise liners mothballed by their owners after new and updated cruise ships replaced them in their fleets. The navy stripped the troop ships down to accommodate more soldiers. The passengers on the passenger ship were new colonists, including business executives, salespersons, engineers, and their families seeking new lives and adventures.

During the four day journey to the Delta Pavonis gateway, Captain Crippin exercised the fighter wings launching them on missions to scout on all sides of the convoy. He also had the pilots practice aggressor and defender maneuvers and simulated combat. As the convoy approached the gateway, the fighters landed in the bays. Then one by one, with *USSP Augusta* in the lead the ships transited the portal in a column.

Two days later, the fleet arrived at Delta

Pavonis 4, with the ships docking at the space station. The colonists debarked at the station to tour the variety of restaurants, shops and the breathtaking view from Delta Pavonis 4. One-thousand of them then shuttled down to start their new lives on the planet. A battalion of nine-hundred soldiers boarded shuttles taking them planetside to augment the garrison.

The other colonists re-boarded the passenger liners for their journeys with the troop ships to Alpha Centauri and Eta Cassiopeiae A and B. *USSP Augusta,* and the frigates *USSP Hepburn,* and *USSP Connole* accompanied them to Alpha Centauri. *USSP Concord, USSP Lang, and USSP Rathburn* provided escorts to Etta Cassiopeiae A and B. Admiral Young granted shore leave to the crews of *USSP Reasoner* and *USSP Bagley*.

Secretary Treat, Emily, Admiral Young, and Captain Crippin took a shuttle to the naval base at Armstrong City. The Base commander Rear Admiral Eugene Cernan invited them to dinner at the Officers' Club. Emily asked Admiral Cernan if his wife Barbara would be attending.

After a pause, he said, "Regrettably no. Barbara left last week to visit with our daughter Teresa on Earth, and to spend time with the grandkids before they are all grown up."

Without missing a beat, Emily said: "Good for her. Our families are so important, and the grandchildren are grown before we know it."

The Admiral then ushered them into the Officers' Club. There they met Vice Admiral Shepard and his wife Louise, who arrived the day before. When the Treat party appeared, Alan Shepard, said, "Mr. Secretary, and Emily, it is so good to see both of you again. As you can see, the Officers' Club is unchanged."

Robert greeted him with a firm handshake, and Emily gave him and Louise warm hugs. Robert then stated, "Alan, let us all dispense with titles. We have been friends and fellow sailors for many years. Emily and I are here to relax before we start on our official missions. Today is the time to celebrate our reunion."

Servers arrived to take drink and appetizer

orders. Louise turned to Emily and said, "Emily your recipes appear to be standard fare at this pub. I am told they all are delicious. Your stamp is throughout the club. Just look around, the animal skins make for decorative rugs and wall hangings. There is not another OC in the service so deliciously decorated.

"The hunting lodge is exquisite and has a particular mixture of a masculine and feminine touch. The framed picture of you and Admiral Scheer with that large cat gets everyone's attention. Your first repeating crossbow is still in its glass case and is a significant attraction.

"I admit I was a bit concerned visiting the dragon cages. However, when I read your plans for the flying reptiles, I became fascinated."

Emily laughed and replied, "Louise, I am so thrilled that the OC kitchen staff kept all the recipes and the decorations. Have you entered the cages? I wonder if the dragons still remember me? Do you hunt or ride the horses?"

Louise replied. "Emily, you are unforgettable, and I am sure the creatures remember you. As for your other question – no, I observed them from the outside of the enclosure.

"I do love to ride but have not hunted. I admire the wildlife but just can't bring myself to kill such exotic animals."

Emily rejoined, "I look forward to riding again. I promise to leave my crossbow behind. We can't let the men have all the fun."

The servers returned to take the dinner order. Alan Shepard asked Emily, "You are the expert here, what do you suggest?"

Emily replied, "My favorite is the cat. However, all the meat is delicious, provided it is not overcooked. Rare or medium rare is the best temperature. The meat tends to get chewy if cooked more than that. The fish is also excellent. The local version of a swordfish is probably the best. Cooking temperatures should be the same as the meat."

The waiters returned with thick slices of steak and fish. Everyone at the table complimented Emily on her suggestions and tastiness of the food.

Louise asked, "Emily do you mind sharing the recipes?"

Emily replied, "By all means. Entrepreneurs are establishing farms to breed the animals as livestock. Commercial fishing fleets harvest the abundant fish. The meat and fish are available on the open market, and are in high demand."

She then called the maitre d' over and instructed, "Ronald, please forward all the recipes to Mrs. Shepard's in-box."

The maitre d' answered: "I will see to it immediately, Mrs. Treat."

Following the meal and another round of drinks, the party moved to a meeting room/lounge in the OC. Three other officers, noting the Admiral's party entering, saluted, excused themselves, and left.

Emily broke the uncomfortable silence when she turned to Admiral Cernan and said, "Admiral, please have your appointment secretary arrange for meetings with the local mayors. I need to evaluate the level of cooperation between the civilian and military governments. I will also need to meet with your recon commander. I have a feeling that the dragons can be valuable in the intelligence gathering operations. Louise and I will leave you gentlemen to your disgusting cigars."

With that, she and Louise made a regal exit.

With the ladies departure, Robert Treat shared President Ford's guidelines for their trip.

"The President requires a first-hand evaluation of the defensive preparations at all the colony worlds. I will evaluate the military aspects and the formation and training of civilian militia units.

"Emily will assess the integration of the colonists into the process, including shelters, stockpiles of food, medicines, medical facilities, transportation, etc. Additionally, Emily will evaluate military uses for the domesticated dragons. She pioneered the domestication process and initiated their physical strengthening to accommodate a human rider. Training them on aerial surveillance should not present difficulties.

"Emily has a team of ecologists who will determine the advisability of introducing trained dragon populations into the other colonial worlds. All of them share a similar climate with Delta Pavonis 4. The ecologists will determine the adaptive evolution of the dragons, and if they can carve out a niche in the ecosystems without significant disruptions. If the experiment fails, the dragons will be collected, removed, or euthanized.

"A successful example of adaptive evolution is when owners of boa-constrictor snakes released them into the Florida Everglades. That ecosystem already had three prime predators, alligators, black bears, and panthers. Over the years a rough equilibrium developed without significant impact on the local ecology. The alligator and constrictor snake populations prey on each other, slowing the increase in numbers. Annual hunting permits cull the excess population.

"Both of us will start with our analysis tomorrow. We are on a tight time schedule and need to report to the President by April. We intend to have our reports on the Presidents desk within the timeframe. Your cooperation is much appreciated. Once we finish here, *Enterprise's* escorts should be back. Shortly after that, we will be on our way to Alpha Centauri, Etta Cassiopeiae A, and B, then on to Beta Hydri 5. There I plan to interview Dr. DiPietro to determine any new developments from the excavations."

One week later, Task Force One departed the space dock. Robert and Emily utilized the transit time to complete rough drafts of their reports.

Chapter 9

Reichstag Building, Berlin, German Empire.

March 15, 1981

After calling an urgent meeting of Parliament, German Chancellor Helmut Schmidt announced the death of Kaiser Wilhelm IV, who died in his sleep following an extended illness. Schmidt declared thirty-days of mourning and also announced the ascension of the Kaiser's third and only surviving son, Crown Prince Albert, to the throne. Albert, currently vacationing in Bora Bora, would return to Berlin as soon as possible. Schmidt announced April 15 as the date for the formal coronation ceremony for Albert I.

Kaiser Wilhelm, who reigned for thirty years, sired three sons. The two older sons died from effects of a mysterious blood disease which debilitated their auto-immune systems. The eldest, William died on April 1, 1978, of pneumonia. His death was followed by Augustus on January 27, 1979, from the flu. With the deaths of two royal brothers, with similar symptoms, physicians at the Berlin Medical Institute tested Albert's blood to determine if the disease was genetic. Negative blood tests' results deepened the mystery.

The fifty-year-old Crown Prince Albert was unmarried and led a playboy lifestyle. With two older brothers, he harbored no aspirations for the throne. Years of dissipation left him in declining health, with frequent bouts of depression. Albert was also rumored to have fathered several illegitimate children. To ensure succession, court officials unsuccessfully tried to arrange a marriage. The dissolute Albert refused to cooperate. The elderly and unwell Kaiser was unable to force the issue. With the Kaiser's death, sixteen-year-old Prince Adolphus Von Hapsburg-Hohenzollern, son of the Emperor of Austria-Hungary Otto von Hapsburg-Lorraine and Empress Alexandria Viktoria Hohenzollern, was next in line to the throne.

Kaiser Wilhelm IV's funeral occurred on March 23, 1981. His remains lay in state on a catafalque under the dome of the Reichstag Building for three days. Millions of Germans filed past honoring their monarch. Citizens of Austria-Hungary, unable to travel to Berlin, left wreaths at the gates of the German Embassy in Vienna. Dignitaries from around the world attended in Berlin. President Gerald Ford and his wife Betty Ford led the American delegation as they paid their respects. Following the ceremony, the funeral procession slowly proceeded to the Charlottenburg Palace Royal Mausoleum for the Kaiser's final internment in an ornate vault alongside prior German Emperors.

On March 25, Chancellor Schmidt convened Parliament. The future of the monarchy was the primary issue. A motion to abolish was overwhelmingly rejected. Several bills were proposed limiting the scope and powers of the monarch. Two days of debate followed and created a bill authorizing a hereditary

Constitutional Monarchy, leaving the Kaiser with only ceremonial responsibilities very similar to those of Queen Elizabeth of England.

Chancellor Schmidt and a delegation from Parliament traveled to Charlottenburg Palace for Kaiser designate Albert 1 to provide Royal Assent. Albert, who never anticipated being Kaiser, and entirely unprepared to rule the German Empire signed the bill into law. The new Crown Prince Adolphus also countersigned, which assured a smooth transition.

On April 15, the day following the mourning period, Kaiser Albert 1 was crowned Kaiser beneath the dome in the Reichstag building. The Kaiser and the Crown Prince rode in an ornate coronation carriage drawn by twelve horses. Troops of cavalry in Prussian Blue uniforms decked out in gold-plated armored breastplates, and gold-plated plumed helmets led and followed the carriage. The procession marched to Charlottenburg Palace where a lavish banquet occurred. Limousines transported the heads of state from numerous countries to the palace. Vice President George H. W. Bush and his wife Barbara led the delegation from the United States.

Robert and Emily Treat were requested as special guests of the Emperor and Empress of Austria-Hungary. Following the banquet, along with Grand Admiral Scheer and his wife, Ingrid, they were invited to stay the weekend at the royal palace in Vienna. There they were formally introduced to Prince Adolphus who was delighted to meet the men who led the fleets that rescued his mother.

On May 15, 1981, following a night of drunken revelry, Albert stumbled and fell down the grand staircase in Charlottenburg Palace, fracturing his skull. He died three hours later. The court physicians diagnosed he suffered a severe heart attack before the fall. A brain hemorrhage sustained from the fall was the cause of death. Chancellor Helmut Schmidt confirmed the cause of death in his official announcement to Parliament. Schmidt proclaimed thirty days of mourning. Crown

Prince Adolphus traveled under escort from Vienna to Berlin to assume his royal mantle.

For the second time in two months, with all due pomp and ceremony, a German Kaiser lay in state under the dome of the Reichstag. Not since the death of Frederick III in 1888 had a royal transition occurred so quickly. Albert's funeral procession slowly marched from the Reichstag to the Charlottenburg Palace Mausoleum to inter the Kaiser's remains.

World leaders witnessed the coronation of Adolphus 1 on June 16 in a joyous event. Robert Treat, Emily Treat, Grand Admiral Scheer, and Ingrid Scheer watched from a place of honor; behind the Austro-Hungarian Emperor and Empress. Following tradition, Adolphus, a young and vibrant man, crowned himself Kaiser of the German Empire.

The coronation rocked the European continent. Kaiser Adolphus was also the heir to the throne of Austria-Hungary. A royal engagement with Princess Josephine of Bohemia was announced two months after the coronation, with the wedding scheduled for April 1982. Children of the royal couple would create a dynasty uniting both of the Central European Germanic empires. With the previous creation of a common market, the successful integration of both national militaries, and significant cultural exchanges, a merger of the governments seemed inevitable.

Chapter 10

September 1, 1981.

Admiral Paulus Jung, aboard his flagship the super dreadnaught *SVS Kaiser Wilhelm IV* with ten escorts, departed Zeta Tucanae's space dock. Equipped with the most modern sensors, and the characteristics of the visitors' portal, the fleet searched for gateways to other solar systems. Five days later, the destroyer *SMS Count Bittenberger* discovered an anomaly, and as she drew closer, a portal opened. Corvette Kaptain Klaus Waldenberg dispatched a drone into the opening and sent a wireless message of the discovery to Admiral Jung.

The drone returned with reports of an orange-red dwarf star, approximately eighty percent of Sol's mass. Jung sent another drone back to scan for potentially habitable planets. Three days later as the fleet assembled at the portal, the probe returned and was rerouted to *SVS Kaiser Wilhelm IV*.

Scientists retrieved the data and began a spectro-analysis of the star and its solar system. Following much debate, the science officers determined the system to be Epsilon Indi, 11.8 light years from Sol.   The second planet in the system, approximately 0.62AU from the primary, was in the habitable zone and showed evidence of an atmosphere. Admiral Jung ordered the fleet to transit into and explore the system. His flagship and two escorts would investigate the second planet, while the balance of the fleet explored the rest of the system.

Two days later *SVS Kaiser Wilhelm IV* and her consorts the frigates *SVS Hamburg*, and *SVS Potsdam,* entered orbit and dispatched drones into the atmosphere. Initial analysis indicated a breathable atmosphere of seventy-six percent nitrogen, twenty-three percent oxygen and numerous trace elements. The planet was fifty-five percent water with oceans separating the significantly forested continents.

Ice covered the polar regions. Significant

glaciation existed but showed evidence of a recent glacial retreat. The northern and southern continental regions evidenced rounded mountainous areas with little vegetation.

Night-time observations indicated substantial volcanic activity and widely scattered pin-pricks of light. Admiral Jung ordered these areas highlighted on the maps, for closer inspection by the drones.

Jung ordered the dispatch of dozens of drones the next morning, focusing on the areas demonstrating illumination. The light sources appeared to be the result of hotspots in fissures situated in previous lava fields. The drones also photographed the potential for significant ruins along the coastal areas and at the junctions of interior rivers.

Jung dispatched shuttles containing science teams and security detachments to the ruins. Ground penetrating radar indicated ruined cities. Core samples noted decayed low-level radioactive materials carbon-dated approximately thirty-thousand years old. The similarities to Beta Hydri were striking. Could this planet be another extinct human world, or could it be a world dominated by the cat-like race? Jung dispatched a drone back to Zeta Tucanae with the findings.

Two days later, the cruiser *SMS Emden* and destroyers *Z30* and *Z41* while searching for other gateways observed activity fifty-thousand miles ahead. Suddenly an unknown portal opened, and three warships emerged. *SMS Emden's* Kapitan Karl Bruner ordered general quarters.

The three intruders IFF transponders quickly identified the warships as *USSP Augusta*, *USSP Connole*, and *USSP Rathburn*. Initially, *Augusta's* Captain James Kellogg also ordered battle stations. Within minutes, the transponder beacons on all the warships relayed positive identification, and a potential incident was averted.

Augusta's Captain James Kellogg wirelessed *Emden's* Kapitan Karl Bruner and exchanged greetings, indicating his squadron transited from Alpha Centauri. Bruner welcomed the American vessels to the Epsilon Indi system, which was recently added to the German-Austro-Hungarian Empire. He also informed Kellogg of the discoveries on Epsilon Indi 2.

Admiral Jung invited the American task force to orbit the planet and send science officers to join in the research. Kellogg accepted the offer. He also dispatched drones to Alpha Centauri and Delta Pavonis describing the new discoveries. In the meantime, while waiting for new orders, the American science teams assisted their German counterparts in the investigation of the ruins.

Washington DC

Secretary of State Haig informed President Ford of the new developments. He advised that it was essential for the President to make an official announcement before the news of the opening of a visitor gateway leading to Alpha Centauri reached the general public. It seemed inevitable that soon the discovery of additional portals would lead to the Sol System.

Ford instructed Haig to set up a meeting with the foreign ministers from the space-faring nations which participated in the mutual defense pact. A united front became more imperative than ever. While the new gateways themselves did not present an imminent danger, they did open additional pathways to invasion.

Two nights later as rumors began to spread, Ford addressed the nation. He placed a positive spin on the discoveries which would facilitate interstellar travel to the various colonial worlds. Ford confirmed the meeting between Haig and the members of the Mutual Defense Pact (MDP), and that no particular action was needed at this time.

Ford also requested additional scientists enlist to go to Beta Hydri 4 to work on those excavations, as the German and many international scientists would be relocating to Epsilon Indi. Initial reports from the Epsilon Indi 2 sites indicated cultural similarities with the ruins at Beta Hydri 4.

He reiterated that the developments themselves did not increase any threat to Earth. To the contrary, knowledge of the portals reduced the risk of a sneak attack. Ford emphasized that the additional gateways allowed for new rapid mutual defense corridors for our allies to provide each other the required support in the event of a conflict.

He also stressed that the portals only facilitated inter-steller travel. It would take several days for an invader fleet to cross the various solar systems between gateways. That timeframe would allow for a meaningful response, and enable the consolidation of allied forces to intercept any invader before they could reach Earth.

Two months later, the Liberian Cruiser *LNS*

Henry Clay escorting two cruise ships on a circuitous journey around the Rings of Saturn reported an anomaly and plotted the location for investigation on the return trip. After delivering the cruise ships to the space station orbiting Titan, The *Clay* returned to the coordinates of the reported anomaly. Suddenly a portal opened. Captain Horace H. Taylor dispatched a drone to the Liberian Defense Platform orbiting Mars, and another into the gateway. Several hours later, the robot ship reappeared indicating the portal led to the Alpha Centauri system.

This gateway presented both opportunity and potential consequences. Earth-based spacecraft now had direct access to the nearest star system. The discovery cut the travel time to those colonies by eighty percent. The new gateway reduced the costs of travel to Alpha Centauri, increasing tourism and immigration. It also opened a shortcut to the Austro-German colonies. Liberia, with its large cruise liner fleets, became the prime beneficiary for new colonists, tourists, and the scientific teams.

The potential consequences involved the German discovery of the visitor portal from Zeta Tucanae into Epsilon Indi. That coupled with the USSP discovery of a visitor portal from Alpha Centauri to Epsilon Indi opened another direct gateway channel into the Sol System.

President Ford directed Secretary of State Schultz to meet with the German Chancellor Helmet Schultz to discuss the issues. With consultations with Austria-Hungary and Liberia, the United States and Liberia agreed to jointly construct Defense platforms on the Sol side of the Alpha Centauri portal. The joint Austro-German Navy would station sufficient fleet forces to defend their two systems. These negotiations strengthened the alliances between the United States, Germany, Austria-Hungary, and Liberia. The nations agreed to expand their consulates in the colonies and schedule regular meetings to coordinate activities.

Chapter 11

August 23, 1984

The Fusion Party's Presidential Convention met in Toronto to nominate their candidate for President. Gerald Ford, responding to his wife Betty's much-publicized addiction to opioid pain medication declined to run for a second term. In 1982, Betty, with the support of her husband, opened the Betty Ford Center in Rancho Mirage, CA for the treatment of addictions. In a well-received speech in February, President Ford made his announcement, citing, "I have achieved my highest aspirations as a politician. It is now time to pass the baton. My duty to our family is to be a fulltime husband and partner with Betty so we can enjoy our children and grandchildren."

During the primaries, Vice President George H.W. Bush won the rematch with Senators Howard Baker, Lowell Weicker, and Robert Dole. During his acceptance speech, Bush personally introduced William Davis, Governor of Ontario, as his selection to be his running mate. The next day the convention nominated Davis by acclamation.

The choice of Davis, who was first elected Governor in 1971, firmly cemented the members of the Parti-Patriote to the Fusion coalition. The ticket included nominees from Texas and Ontario which tied the party together geographically.

Bush and Davis crisscrossed the country east to west and north to south. They pushed the Fusionist platform of prosperity, a clean environment, industrial growth, expanding colonies, and an increasingly powerful defense program. The less than three percent unemployment rate caused employers to hike wages and increase their benefits programs to attract and retain qualified employees.

The Republicans convened their convention on August 10 in Dallas, TX. Philip Crane was nominated on the first ballot. Crane won hard-fought primary battles with other conservative firebrands Philip Graham from Texas and Senator Pete Wilson from California. Crane chose Wilson for his running mate, hoping to win California's electoral votes.

The Republicans were encouraged by their mid-term election success in 1982 when they won four Senate, and ten House seats at the expense of the Social Democrat Party, which was still reeling from the terrorist acts in 1980. Crane and Wilson campaigned vigorously. Their platform stressed a return to conservative values and to curb growing budget deficits.

The Social Democrat candidates included Chicago Mayor Jessie Jackson, Senators Walter Mondale, Frank Church, John Kennedy, Jerry Brown, Gary Hart, and Governor Jimmy Carter. Gary Hart used his charisma and eloquent speaking style to jump off as the front-runner. He built up a substantial delegate lead in the early primaries. Hart's candidacy received a significant boost when Kennedy dropped out following the Oregon Primary and endorsed him. Hart clinched the nomination when he defeated Brown in the California Primary.

The Democrats held their convention on July 16 in San Francisco. The vice presidency was the only question to be settled. Hart kept his selection secret until his acceptance speech. Towards the end of his address, he announced Robert Kennedy as his choice for running mate. To thunderous applause, Kennedy made his way to the platform where they joined raised arms. The next day Kennedy's name was placed into nomination. The convention confirmed him by acclamation. The ticket was nicely balanced including Hart from Colorado and Kennedy from Massachusetts.

Hart and Kennedy, both charismatic candidates, attracted large crowds at their campaign stops. The Social Democrat platform highlighted government control of healthcare, the railroads, and a national retirement pension program to provide a guaranteed income level for all retired persons.

The elections held on November 6, 1984, the

Fusion ticket of Bush and Davis won fifty percent of the vote, carrying forty-nine states and receiving a total of four hundred and eighteen electoral votes. They also retained their majorities in the House and Senate.

The Republicans won thirty-five percent of the vote and one hundred and Seventy-three electoral votes. They were victorious in eleven states including Arizona, Baja, Cuba, Dominica, Illinois, New Mexico, Puerto Rico, New York, and Pennsylvania. They also won the three votes in the District of Columbia.

The Social Democrats won fourteen percent of the vote and fifty-two electoral votes. They were victorious in Colorado, Massachusetts, Minnesota, New Hampshire, Oregon, and Washington.

On January 21, 1985, the Presidential Inauguration ceremony needed to be moved inside the Capitol Rotunda as the outside temperature was seven degrees, with a minus twenty-five-degree windchill factor. Chief

Justice Warren Burger administered the Presidential Oath of Office to George H.W. Bush, and the former Associate Justice Potter Stewart administered the Vice Presidential Oath to William Davis. Sitting in seats of honor behind the Presidential party was the new Secretary of State Casper Weinberger with his wife Jane and the new Secretary of Defense Robert Treat and Emily.

Chapter 12

March 1, 1985.

Moscow, Russia

Andrei Gromyko, following his second heart attack, tendered his resignation pending the selection of his successor. He then nominated his close confidant Mikhail Gorbachev to be General Secretary of the Socialist Party. On March 11, the Congress of Peoples Deputies confirmed the nomination, and on March 15, the deputies elected Gorbachev to the position of President of Russia.

In response to Molotov's congratulations letter, one of Gorbachev's first initiatives was an attempt to improve relations with the Bolsheviks in Soviet Russia.   He offered glasnost by offering to negotiate a treaty recognizing each country's existence and confirming the current borders. On August 1, Gorbachev and Molotov met in Geneva,

Switzerland, to sign the agreement, formally ending the civil war, ushering in perestroika between the nations and an exchange of ambassadors.

With full diplomatic relations came economic trade particularly in food, which alleviated the persistent food shortages plaguing both nations. The trans-Siberian railroad reopened providing an efficient way to move goods and industrial products between the two countries.

Together, the Russian countries opened negotiations with the Far Eastern Republic and Japan to provide the reopening of the railroad to Vladivostok. This enabled the Japanese to sell industrial goods to both Russias, which enabled the expansion of free trade through the co-prosperity sphere. Additional trade negotiations allowed Japanese products into Western Europe through Ukraine and the German and Austro-Hungarian Empires.

The European nations welcomed the end of the Russian Civil war, as there was always the potential for the conflict involving other countries. The advantages of access to additional markets became a great opportunity, and they seized the chance to open another trade route to the far east.

Chapter 13

Constantinople, Greece

The opening of commerce between Europe and the far east became an enormous economic plus for the Greek Kingdom of the Hellenes. Since the culmination of the Greco-Turkish war in 1923, Hellenic Greece consisted of western Anatolia, Thrace, including the Dardanelles, the Bosphorus, the Aegean Islands, and Crete. King Constantine 1 moved the Hellenic seat of government to Constantinople, relegating Athens to a regional capital city.

The acquisitions provided them with control of the Aegean Sea, the narrow Dardanelles, and the Bosphorus Straits, which was the only seaborne traffic lane between the Mediterranean and the Black Sea. As these were Hellenic territorial waters, Greece collected tolls from all shipping passing from the Mediterranean into and exiting from the Black Sea. In 1960, The United Kingdom which previously ruled Cyprus, in a treaty ceded the island to the Hellenes in return for elimination of the tolls to British shipping interests.

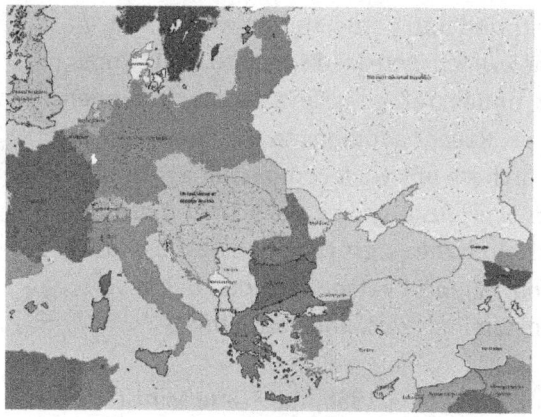

Hellenic Greece

The Greek-Hellenic Navy dominated the Aegean and Black seas, and actively patrolled in the eastern Mediterranean Sea. The navy consisted of three of the former United States Navy fusion powered Dakota class battleships, HS Hydra, HS Spetai, and HS Psana. The Navy honored the memory of their first ironclad battleships by reusing their historic names for the new fast battleships.

Additionally, the four pre-dreadnaught Mississippi class battleships were extensively modernized into battlecruisers with fusion engines which increased speed to thirty knots, radar, antiaircraft guns, and electronic gunnery control. Recent additions to the fleet included the purchase of two decommissioned United States Navy fusion powered Ticonderoga Class attack aircraft carriers renamed *HS Elli and HS Athena*. Support vessels included destroyers, cruisers, minelayers, and patrol boats.

On September 16, 1985, the Prime Minister of Greece, Constantine Karamanlis convened the Ministerial Council in an urgent meeting to discuss the threats of the President of Turkey, Kenan Evren. President Evren, a Turkish nationalist who took power in a military coup in 1980, resented the sudden Hellenic windfall in toll revenues from the increase in shipping traffic, in what previously were Turkish controlled waters. He was determined to recapture all of the Anatolia provinces lost to the Greeks in 1923. That also would provide Turkey with one-half of the revenue stream.

President Evren used the excuse of violence and vandalism against Muslim Mosques in Cyprus by radical members of the Greek Orthodox Church to launch a surprise invasion of the island. Twenty thousand Turkish soldiers landed with tanks and armored personnel carriers. With approximately thirty-five percent of the island's population being Turkish nationals, the invading force received significant support.

The next day, informed of the Turk invasion of Cyprus, Constantine Karamanlis presented a Declaration of War against Turkey to King Constantine II, who immediately signed the document. The General Staff ordered The Hellenic Navy including two of the Dakota battleships *HS Hydra, HS Spetai* and the attack aircraft carrier *HS Elli* with troop transports and escorts to steam towards Cyprus with a relief force. The orders were to destroy the Turkish Navy stationed off Cyprus and land the relief troops.

However, the Turkish invasion was only a feint. As the Hellenic relief force neared Cyprus, the Turkish Army launched two land-based attacks, one towards Constantinople, the other towards Smyrna. Their airforce bombed Hellenic ground positions and military installations. The Hellenic border fortifications held up the Turkish advance for several days providing the Hellenes time to mobilize their army. Slowly, under a constant Turkish artillery barrage, the Hellenic defenses were reduced to rubble. The Turks massed their troops for the push to the sea.

The Hellenic officers stationed at their orbiting defense platform, in synchronous orbit over the Aegean, could observe the potential breakthroughs by the Turks. The station was realigned so that the laser batteries and rail guns pointed towards the battlefields. Early in the morning, the Turkish cannons began bombarding the crumbling fortifications.

Using the flashes of the cannon fire as markers, the defense platform began an orbital

bombardment of the Turkish artillery positions. Fires from exploding munitions provided adequate illumination for the rail guns to concentrate their kinetic strikes on the massed troop and tank formations.
Daylight revealed the devastation in and around the Turkish formations which turned the battlefields into wastelands.

Reinforcements to the Hellenic Armies counter-attacked driving the Turks back over the borders, closely harassing the Turk armies as they fell back. The Orbital bombardment continued to rain down on the retreating soldiers and support facilities including Turkish airfields and naval installations along the Mediterranean and the Black Sea coasts.

The Hellenic Navy battlecruisers *HS Lemnos, HS Kilkis, HS Troas,* and *HS Smyrna* led a task force which patrolled the Black Sea coast of Anatolia, landing troops to invest the port city Trebizond, and shelling the retreating Turkish army with their twelve-Inch guns. The retreat turned into a rout. However, for the trapped army there was no place to run to or hide from the terror which rained on them from above.

Satellite pictures from other nations flooded the internet. The Turkish armies faced virtual annihilation from an unseen enemy. Protests against the orbital strikes and threats of economic sanctions from Germany, Austria-Hungary, France, Italy, and the United Kingdom were first rejected by the Hellenic government as they were just defending themselves from an unprovoked attack.

The United States did not get involved in the sanctions, as the war was viewed as a local European issue. President Bush did offer to send Secretary of State Weinberger to mediate an end of the war. Following a meeting with Weinberger, Prime Minister Karamanlis announced an agreement to a European brokered cease-fire in western Anatolia. Karamanlis also consented to send a delegation to Geneva where the European Powers would facilitate a peace conference.

The fighting continued in Cyprus with conventional weapons. The Hellenes landed over thirty-thousand troops. The Navy reinforced the fleet with a task force escorting *HS Psara* and *HS Athena* which brought another eighty aircraft into the engagement zone. With local Turkish air and naval bases destroyed by the orbital bombardment, Hellenic warbirds dominated the sky.

Sensors aboard the orbital defense platform detected three Turkish submarines threatening the Hellenic naval units. Destroyers, directed to the specific areas, depth charged the subs, sinking one, and forcing the others to surface and surrender.

On Cyprus itself, civilian casualties grew as the Turk Army entrenched itself in prior residential areas. Surrounded, under constant bombardment, cut off from reinforcements and supplies, the Turk commanding General Osman Pasha requested terms for a cease-fire. Wishing to minimize civilian casualties on both sides the Hellenic commander General Constans

Pelogise agreed to a meeting attended by senior officers from both sides. At the conclusion, the Hellenes and the Turks announced a cease-fire.

The treaty of Geneva signed on October 30, 1985, ended the war as status quo antebellum with no border changes. The Hellenic army retreated from the captured territory in Anatolia. The Turks evacuated their troops from Cyprus abandoning all the equipment and agreed to pay five billion dollars in reparations over five years.

Over one-half of the Turkish residents of Cyprus elected to immigrate to the mainland, as they feared reprisals because they collaborated with the invading forces. Approximately one-third of the reparations were allocated for the relocation and resettlement costs. The ethnic Turk Cypriots who elected to remain obtained assurances of civil and religious rights by the Hellenic government.

The war demonstrated the destructive power of

orbital defense platforms when directed against land-based armies. It was a sobering indication that in any conflict with an interstellar opponent, control of the orbitals began with system-wide defenses.   The major powers realized that an invader needed to be destroyed or substantially damaged before and after they transited from the gateways. Once an aggressor controlled the orbital space, their victory was virtually assured. Gateway defense became a priority.

Chapter 14

Visitor Gateway Beta Hydri

February 15, 1987

The drone stationed at the gateway on the far side of the Mu Cassiopeiae system transmitted that an alien probe just entered, traveling at .3 C and was on a predicted course for the Beta Hydri portal. Two days later, the probe exited the Beta Hydri gate, set a course directly for Beta Hydri 4, and within three hours began to transmit an encrypted audio and video message utilizing the encryption formula in use at the time of the original fly by.

The station computers recognized the encryption sequence and began to decode it into an English translation. The communication officer brought the data directly to the base commander Captain Michael J Smith, USSP. Upon reading the message and viewing the video, Captain Smith ordered it re-encrypted to the highest level and transmitted to Vice Admiral Shepard at Delta Pavonis. Shepard, after seeing the deciphered message, placed the USSP on alert, then re-transmitted the missive to Washington, DC.

February 16, 1987

Washington, DC – White House

President Bush assembled his Security Council in the White House Situation Room. Attendees included: Vice President William Davis, Chief of Staff James Baker, the Secretary of State, Casper Weinberger, Secretary of Defense Robert Treat, the Attorney General, Edwin Meese, The Secretary of Homeland Security, Donald Regan, and the National Security Advisor, Lt. General Colin Powell.

Bush began, "You all need to view this video before we can start the discussion. The critical information contained makes this the most crucial event of the twentieth century, and likely in the world to date. It includes a message from our possible human ancestors which is both a greeting and an appeal for assistance, a virtual request for an alliance against what they term a vicious common enemy."

With that prelude, President Bush sat down, the lights dimmed, and the video started.

The first scene showed an official seal illustrating the surface of a planet orbiting a gas giant with multiple rings and several smaller moons. The lettering on intertwined ribbons surrounding the seal was illegible. The image faded into the background, and a human male wearing a military-style uniform walked to the center. The man appeared to be nearly eight feet tall and quite slender. He featured a high hairless forehead, broad cheekbones, narrow lips, and an almost pointed chin. As he began speaking, it was apparent that he was talking in his native language, simultaneously translated into English.

He stated, *"Greetings to Earth, the home of our long lost children. My name, loosely translated into your writing is Garand Minion. I am the supreme commander of our military situated on a close neighbor in the constellation you call Andromeda. You have named our planetary system Upsilon Andromedae. We reside on a large moon, approximately twice the size of Earth, orbiting a gas giant, which is the fourth planet from our star. With your outward expansion, it became inevitable that we would meet. That is why I was delegated to establish the first contact with our descendants.*

"Our civilization began in the middle of what you call the Milky Way. We were expansionists, settling inhabitable planets wherever we traveled. We first colonized your world over forty-thousand of your years ago.

"Your planet was much colder at that time, with what you call glaciers covering much of your northern hemisphere and the mountains throughout. We settled on the coastal plains in what you term the tropics. From images scanned from the data obtained from our past visits, it is evident that your climate warmed, and the glaciers melted. All traces of our

civilization now lie under your oceans.

"Our colonists encountered three primitive human species in your world. The inhabitants began to serve us, and in return, we brought civilization to the natives. It was inevitable that we co-mingled with the natives and created a hybrid race. It is very possible that over time all of them merged into one.

"All our colonization ended when our expansion encountered a very warlike race named the Krieg. We intermittently fought with them for supremacy for thousands of your years. Those wars were galaxy wide, some of the battles occurred on and near your planet. Thousands of ago we decided to abandon your world and others in that sector. However, many of our people chose to stay.

"Eventually, the Krieg wars transitioned from supremacy to extermination. We no longer fought for conquest but focused on annihilation. Both races developed weapons which rendered planets to be uninhabitable. Eventually, the

Krieg disappeared into the core of the galaxy. For thousands of years, we watched and waited for them to return. Ultimately, we destroyed our weapons of mass destruction. However, war became a part of our society. Without the common enemy, we turned on each other, devastating ourselves. Our society fractured, and we sank into a dark age.

"Several thousand of your years ago, we finally made peace with each other and determined that disarmament was the best path, with only the planetary police bearing arms. That policy served us well until over one-thousand years ago when the Krieg returned. At first, neither side wanted to renew the wars, and an uneasy co-existence prevailed. We rebuilt our fleets and recreated our armies. Predictably, hostile incidents escalated into war.

"We are more numerous and occupy more systems. However, our violent tendencies and fighting capabilities eroded during the thousands of years of peace. The Krieg, as warlike as ever, captured several of our

planetary systems, converting the inhabitable worlds into hunting preserves for their upper caste warriors. Humans, reduced to savages, created primitive weapons to resist the hunters. The Kreig also bio-engineered their DNA, then infused various implants into our captured young, creating a hybrid race called Kriegsters; who became a lower caste of warriors, led by the Krieg. Every year they turn the ablest of the captive children into their fighters. Those who fail the test are enslaved or exiled to the hunting preserves."

Displaying images of the Kriegsters, Minion demonstrated they were humanoid with foreheads extending up to two inches over their eyes with implants located next to their eyes and extending behind their ears.

"The Kriegsters are programmed with savagery and follow orders without question. They show no mercy to our combatants and very little to our civilians. It is challenging to fight against your altered progeny. After years of stalemate, we are beginning to suffer losses in this war.

"Our examination of data scans indicates your planet has a warlike past. We need your warriors, as we are facing the danger that the Krieg will split our planetary systems. If that happens, they will open a pathway to your occupied worlds and inevitably to Earth.

"It is highly likely that the Krieg knows of your existence and will view you as an enemy. We offer you an alliance to counter this mutual threat. Our probe will remain in your Beta Hydri system for an answer. It is programmed to respond to requests asked in my name. If you decide to seek an agreement, the robot will provide your delegation coordinates to the portals leading to our planet to negotiate a formal alliance."

A stunned silence ensued following the end of the video. Bush looked around at his security council.

He then said, "We all were aware that this could happen. It seems to be fortunate that our human neighbors found us first. We have the time to meet with our space-faring partners to determine if they will ally with us in helping the Andromedans fight the Krieg. If we fail to do that, the Krieg will undoubtedly find us unprepared."

Looking at Secretary Weinberger, Bush requested his input.

Weinberger replied, "I will set up meetings with the other space powers, emphasizing that the video needs to be translated into German, French, Italian, and Japanese, with copies of the original English version included in the packages. I am confident that the Brits, German / Austro – Hungarians, Australians, and Liberians will be on board. I suspect the Hellenes will go along with the German / Austro – Hungarians. I think the French and Italians will come, also. The Japanese fleet is an unknown quantity. It is possible they will decide to defend their own systems. "

Secretary Treat was the next to speak. He said, "I would like to be part of the delegation to

Andromeda. My military experience will allow me to evaluate their offensive and defensive capabilities. I also want to understand the tactics and skills of the Krieg.

"The defense platforms protecting Earth are armed and ready. Two new platforms guard the gateway leading from the Sol System to Alpha Centauri. That, coupled with the two platforms protecting the Delta Pavonis portal and the Home Fleet, backing up both should adequately protect the main entrances to Sol.

"We have thirty-five super dreadnaughts ready for deployment. Five of them are undergoing a refit at the Earth and Moon space docks. Three others are in the same situation at the Mars dock. All can be completed within two weeks. The Liberians launched their second dreadnaught last week, and it's conducting its shakedown cruise. They, with their cruiser escorts, will be available to defend Mars.

"We currently have seven-thousand warbirds deployed both on the warships, moons, defense platforms, and planet based. We can notify the various defense contractors to ramp up production. It is likely we will soon be going to war. We will need replacements of fighters, bombers, and weaponry. With your permission, I will notify the commanders of the military academies to emphasize pilot applications, and make preparations to increase flight training."

Bush nodded his assent and said: "Robert, make your plans."

Looking at Attorney General Meese, Bush stated, "Ed, dust off those preparations for martial law in case we need to defend Earth and the United States."

Addressing Secretary Regan and General Powell, Bush stated, "Gentlemen, I need plans for the defense of the homeland. Make any revisions you need for the current preparations, and update Jim with any changes."

Then addressing the entire security council, Bush stated, "Gentlemen, we all have our assignments, let's get to it. I have to prepare a speech to the nation. I want your proposals for a positive response back to Jim within twenty-four hours so he and I can prepare my message before I break the news to the public."

Chapter 15

February 22, 1987

Geneva, Switzerland

The summit meeting of the space powers commenced at 9 am. The President of the Swiss Confederation, Pierre Aubert presided over the meeting.

Attending dignitaries included Casper Weinberger, Robert Treat, Foreign Minister Hans-Dietrick Gencher of Germany, and Vice Chancellor Alois Mock of Austria-Hungary. Other delegations included Foreign Secretary Sir Geoffrey Howe of Great Britain, Crown Prince Akihito of Japan, Secretary of State Jean Francis-Pomcet of France, Foreign Minister Giglio Andreotti of Italy, Minister of Foreign Affairs William Haydon of Australia, and Secretary of State Reginald Taylor of Liberia.

Greece, India, and Brazil also sent lower-level

delegations, as their fleets only consisted of patrol vessels. However, they would play an essential role in Earth's defense, as they had well-armed orbital platforms.

President Aubert began the meeting, thanking all the attendees and reminding them that all of the nation's governments had previously viewed the Andromedan's video. Humanity was now acutely aware that their original assumptions of a potentially far distant risk were no longer valid. The real crisis was upon them. Decisions of how to address the threat, and which nation would lead the response needed to be made.

Following much discussion, the general consensus agreed that a delegation should travel to Upsilon Andromedae to meet with their potential allies and determine if an accord could be reached. As the United States possessed the biggest fleet and the gateways to Andromeda lay in its territory, the delegates decided The United States Space Patrol would lead the response. Each of the other nations would provide warships. The size and strength of the significant space power's fleets would determine how many battleships each country would send. As the United States Navy fielded the most massive space fleet, the USSP would send three; with two each from the Austro-Germans, British and Japanese. Australia, France, Italy, and Liberia would each provide one. The convoy escorts would represent all the attending nations. Following the session, the senior representative from all the countries signed the letter of intent. Within one week, the accord was ratified by each government.

Following the signing of the document, President Bush directed that Vice Admiral Shepard be promoted to a four-star Fleet Admiral, as he would be leading a multi-national flotilla to Upsilon Andromedae 4. Treat dispatched the CNO to Delta Pavonis 4 to formalize the promotion and deliver the new assignment.

Shepard humbly accepted the assignment, then composed a reply to the Andromeda probe that he would be commanding the escort for a delegation that would travel to Andromadae 4 to negotiate an alliance. He also listed the anticipated size of the fleet and types of warships. Shepard also included a file which contained the language dictionaries from the representative governments.

The robot acknowledged receipt of the messages and responded with the coordinates to the gateways. It then broke orbit, ignited its engines, and sped away for the return to its home system.

Chapter 16

March 13, 1987

Beta Hydri 4

The arrival of the Japanese task force, under the command of Prince Hitachi, the younger brother to Crown Prince Akihito, completed the international flotilla. He flew his flag on the super dreadnaught *IJN Yamato* and traveled in consort with its sister ship *IJN Musashi*.

The balance of the international force orbiting Beta Hydri 4 included the super dreadnaughts *USSP Texas, USSP California, USSP New York, SMS Bismark, SMS Tirpitz, HMS King George VI, HMS Queen Elizabeth*, the Australian *HMAS Melbourne,* the French *Richelieu*, the Italian *Littorio*, and the Liberian *LNS Monrovia*. The forty-two escorts of the capital ships included ten cruisers, fifteen destroyers, and seventeen frigates. The size of the convoy was intended to demonstrate to the Andromedans the potential of Earth's defensive and offensive capabilities.

That evening Admiral Shepard and Robert Treat hosted the international task force commanders and their civilian government representatives to a reception in the Officers Club in the defense platform. There, Scheer and Treat held court as they reminisced about their past successes battling the Russian pirates, their hunting expeditions on Delta Pavonis 4, and the taming of the dragons.

Following the reception, Treat, and Shepard scheduled separate meetings in the club conference rooms.

Treat met with cabinet ministers from the various countries. The first order of business was to select a leader. His colleagues chose Treat to be the government's spokesperson. They considered him to hold the most prestige as he was a retired Vice Admiral, was victorious in space battles, and now the United States Secretary of Defense. He agreed to consult with them on all decisions.

Treat then rose and said, "It is my understanding that all of you were provided plenipotentiary powers to negotiate for your respective governments. That is important, as the Andromedan planetary governments represent a united people. They are unfamiliar to several political, and sometimes competing entities on a single planet. Your governments have entrusted you with these powers, and we must all use them wisely. We need to be coordinated in our negotiations."

Across the hall, Shepard held his meeting. Attending officers included: Prince Hitachi, Grand Admiral Heinrich Scheer of the Austro-German Navy, First Sea Lord of the British Royal Navy, Sir William Stavely, Admiral Francois Picard from France, Admiral Guiseppe Mareno from Italy, and Admiral Horace H. Taylor from Liberia.

Shepard began by saying, "Each of our governments and military forces will have different roles to play. Prince Hitachi sits on the Emperor's Council. The Grand Admiral and Sir

William are cabinet members of their respective governments. Francois, Guiseppe, and Horace are high ranking Admirals for their respective navies.

"The Andromedans have experience in battling the Krieg and should be able to provide valuable lessons. However, the guiding principles must be an equal partnership in any alliance. By their own admission, they are losing the war. They need us as much as we will need them.

"Your governments selected me to be the military leader of this mission. In that capacity, I have plans to exercise our crews during our over two weeks journey to Andromadae 4 The goal is to create a unified fighting unit. Each day the escorts from different nations will take the point position of our column. As we pass through each portal, the lead ship will send a drone back indicating the system status, then we will follow. The position of the dreadnaughts will also change daily, with the captain of the lead dreadnaught being the officer of the day. We will also conduct simulations of the ship to ship combat. Battle station drills will be done on a random basis.

"The fighter wings will war game alternating between combat air patrol and aggressors. The laser batteries will be set on minimal. If a warbird is locked on in the targeting system and lit up by the laser, it is considered shot down. It will then leave the exercise area.

"The aggressors will also make bombing runs on the warships. If point defense locks on to a fighter, it is out of the action. After action reports will highlight what went right, and what didn't. We will learn from our mistakes, and we all will be better warriors because of those lessons.

"The purpose of this is to be ready for combat at all times. You are free to keep score, and you likely will. After all, healthy competition brings out the best in us. However, the scorecard is not the ultimate focus of this exercise. It is essential that we develop mutual cooperation in attitude and tactical coordination in action.

That is why I will often mix up the warbird squadrons, so we learn to work together. While we are on a mission to create an alliance, we could potentially be entering into harm's way. We must be ready."

PART TWO - ANDROMEDA

Chapter 17

Andromeda 4

Supreme Commander Garand Minion exited the airlock from his shuttle into the Karonele defense platform. He was there to determine the readiness of the crew to face the Krieg who were advancing ever closer. The Home was the largest frontier world and recently upgraded the strong system's defenses, which included six defense platforms and a powerful fleet.

On the way to his headquarters, he paused then entered the observation dome to view the alpha sunrise as it rose above the giant gas planet Omegatron. The view was magnificent, illuminating Omegatron and its dozens of smaller satellites.

The star system, called Home, resided in a binary system. The alpha star a bright white sun had a distant red dwarf companion. Eons ago, Omegatron captured their homeworld Aurora, which was pushed out of its orbit and plunged towards the alpha star following the collision of two nearby planets. Omegatron's gravity field pulled Aurora into a stable orbit, preventing it from becoming a burned rock.

The capture led to untold millions of years of tectonic upheaval and volcanic activity. Those factors, combined with the heat from the alpha star which melted the frozen oceans, formed a stable nitrogen/oxygen atmosphere favorable for the formation of an ecosystem. Over seventy-five thousand years ago, the first explorers arrived. The subsequent colonists built a civilization, which at first populated the solar system, and then continued their star travels.

The Home system was in danger for the first time in over thirty-thousand years. The defeat inflicted on an arch-enemy, the Krieg, in a titanic battle, stopped the Krieg before they could destroy the system. Home's fleets pursued their retreating foe and brought them to action seven transits away, where the Krieg fleet was annihilated. However, the thousands of years of peace were over, and war was drawing near. Garand's reveries were interrupted by the beep of his com unit. He was needed at the command center immediately.

Upon his arrival, the officer of the day handed him a decoded message. The Triberbrow System, five transits away was under assault. The Krieg fleets were sustaining significant losses navigating the portal's protective minefields and were being engaged by the defense platforms. The gateway's defense fleet was moving into position in preparation for a counterattack. The lasered message, traveling between gateways at light speed was already three days old.

Garand realized that the battle for Triberbrow was likely already decided. However, he prepared a relief fleet to assist if needed. One of his academy classmates, and a close friend, Piercley Commetriez, commanded Triberbrow's defense forces. If the system were likely to fall, Piercley, if still alive, would withdraw his surviving fleets.

Garand assembled a fleet of twenty battleships and fifty support vessels and assigned it to his second in command, Trulegy Netscomb. Minion instructed Netscomb to the transit into the next system one gateway away, as there were three potential portals located there leading to Triberbrow from Home. Garand also ordered the gateway defenses to send fast frigates and escorts to look for retreating defense forces down those pathways. If none were found, the ships should travel to Triberbrow and determine if the defenders successfully repelled the invasion.

Netscomb was instructed to wait for the anticipated scouting reports. Garand instructed Trulegy to render any needed aid to retreating Andromedan warships and to lay ambushes for any pursuing Krieg squadrons.

That left Garand with fifty battleships and two-hundred support vessels to defend the Home system. Presuming that the Krieg were victorious during Triberbrow fleet battles, they would need time to consolidate their gains by defeating the planetary armies and repairing damaged warships before moving forward.

For far too long, the Andromeda fleets fought a defensive war anticipating that the Krieg offensive would grind to a halt for lack of supplies and repair facilities. Somehow, the Krieg changed the equation and were able to self-sustain their invasion. Garand decided to find out how and intended to take the initiative away from the Krieg.

Chapter 18

Triberbrow System

As the Krieg warships began to pour through the gateway, they ran into a nuclear bomb layered minefield. The first ships through were cruiser and frigate class vessels which exploded in fiery holocausts as the programmed mines accelerated to detonate at close proximity. The following warships, observing the devastation began firing their point defense weapons into the minefield. Still, dozens of them were destroyed.

The battleships followed into the carnage caused by the thinning minefields. Four of them exploded, and several others sustained significant damage until the mines expended themselves.

The four defense platforms then began to fire their powerful laser type weapons. The damaged battleships and several new entrants were destroyed. While the battleships engaged the defenses, the Triberbrow warships, including twenty battleships, attacked. The battle lasted several hours before the concentrated fire from the overwhelming number of Krieg battleships destroyed the platforms, and caused the surviving Triberbrow warships to retreat.

As the last Krieg battleships passed through the gateway, the wreckage of over sixty Krieg warships, the defense platforms, and ten Triberbrow vessels drifted through space. Even with their heavy losses, the Krieg fleet still contained sixty battleships.

Supreme Commander Commetriez watched the battle unfold from his command center on the largest of five defense platforms defending the planet. He was disappointed that the Krieg sent their smaller warships through first. That was a change from their previous tactics. He hoped to destroy more of their capital ships with the minefield. Over ten-thousand of his warriors perished in the failed defense of the gateway. Fleet losses included two of his scarce capital ships destroyed and four others severely damaged.

Contingency plans for an evacuation were implemented. Still, Commetriez was cautiously optimistic. His support vessels were busy laying new minefields, and his fleet contained thirty battleships. Four others were nearing completion in the shipyards.

The next day, his optimism evaporated. The Krieg were reinforced with ten new capital ships and thirty escorts. An immediate evacuation of the government and as many as possible of the population was in order. Shuttles brought the government officials and tens of thousands of civilians up to the shipyards to be loaded onto the four incomplete battleships. Private and commercial vessels were commandeered to evacuate many thousands of other refugees. As each ship was filled, it departed towards the central gateway towards the Home System. The last to leave included the incomplete warships plus ten frigate class escorts.

The remaining population entered long convoys taking them to prepared shelters dug inside the mountains Those too far away to travel were sequestered with their families in the subterranean sections of the cities. As is inevitable, rioting and looting took place in the cities. The police chiefs were instructed to shoot the rioters and looters on sight and focus their efforts on protecting the sheltered population. Civil order needed to be maintained for as long as possible.

Commetriez consulted with his friend and army commander, General Rigaloggo Akramaguian, about the protection of the planet. Akramaguian ordered his ground forces to enter the military's prepared defensive positions, built to withstand an orbital bombardment.   He would direct the defense from the planetary command center deep within a mountain. Hardened laser batteries would attack Krieg warships in orbit. Concealed anti-ship missiles and laser batteries were made ready to attack the landing craft containing Krieg soldiers.

After pausing two days to repair the damaged warships, and receive the reinforcements, the Krieg began their advance towards Triberbrow Prime. Their fleet advanced in three columns with the escort vessels in a screen to the front, followed by the cruisers, then the battleships. It would be at least four hours before the engagement would begin.

Commetriez transferred his flag to the most massive battleship, T1911, and then scheduled a video conference with General Akramaguian, the fleet captains, and the defense platform commanders.

He began, "We all know that the Krieg fleet outnumbers us more than two to one in battleships. They are advancing in three columns. I suspect the wing columns are to circle around behind us to cut off any retreat.

"Our stealth minefields should reduce the Krieg superior numbers. Anticipating that the Krieg will deploy their smaller vessels out front, I directed our technical staff to program the mines to stay in stealth mode until the warships smaller than a heavy cruiser pass through the field. Then the mines will activate and detonate close to the most significant enemy vessel.

"As their capital ships approach the minefields, all our warships will launch their missiles at the approaching battleships and cruisers, and sprint missiles at the escorts. The confusion caused by the multi-layers of counter-measures should allow much of the minefields to go undetected until they detonate. The Krieg battleships can sustain two or three mine explosions. Four or five should destroy them or put them out of action. Once the minefields detonate, my center command will advance at full throttle through the escorts to create a ship to ship melee, hopefully minimizing their advantage in superior firepower. Once we are fully engaged, Wings A and B will attack the flanking columns with the objective to prevent an envelopment.

"Any of the Krieg center warships which manage to get by my forces will be confronted by the defense platforms which are the planets last line of protection. Hit them first with the missiles, then unload on them with the lasers."

Then directing his comments to the platform commanders, he said, "Coordinate with General Akramaguian. He will support you with his ground-based lasers. Paint any of the Krieg's vessels you are unable to target yourselves, he will deal with them."

Then addressing all of his commanders Commetriez stated, "Always realize, if we don't survive this battle, it is a great honor to die defending your system, planet, and families. Today is a good day to do so, just kill as many of them as you can first."

Chapter 19

Battle of Triberbrow Prime

The Krieg armada majestically swept forward towards the Triberbrow fleet drawn up to defend the planet. The alpha male commanding the center column of battleships exclaimed that his pride of warriors would be the first to claim the world. He called the Triberbrow soldiers cowards for hiding behind their defenses. Their people would soon be food or slaves.

His confidence continued even as the defenders launched thousands of missiles. After all, his interceptor missiles, counter-measures, and point defense batteries would negate the attack. He ordered his fleet to fire volleys of rockets at the defenders. Suddenly, his battleship shook from multiple nearby nuclear explosions. Damage reports multiplied indicating numerous hull breaches and uninhabitable radiated portions of the vessel.

Two of his six reactors were off-line reducing his speed. Multiple ruptured power conduits took down his primary weapons. The alpha male exhorted his engineers to complete the repairs, as he would not be denied his victory. Suddenly, his communications officer received messages from the entire fleet. The enemy battleships were closing the range and would soon be engaging ship to ship. This battle was rapidly descending to a fight at knifepoint range. He screamed to his chief engineer that he wanted the weapons back online now!

Commetriez, sitting in his command chair had a look of grim satisfaction on his face. During the missile exchange, his column lost three battleships, one destroyed and two others damaged and floating helplessly, out of action. The Krieg sustained more than a dozen destroyed or damaged battlewagons. Most of the destruction was due to the mines. The numbers were evening out, and he had the initiative. As the confused battle lines merged, a massive damaged Krieg battleship closed into range.

Commetriez commanded, "Fire all forward and starboard batteries into that ship."

The alpha male viewed the closing enemy battleship with trepidation. Only one-half of his weapons were operational, and the numerous hull breaches were attractive targets. His warship trembled as the lasers tore additional holes into its hull. He felt several secondary explosions deep inside his ship, then conduits exploded around him as the main power failed. Emergency lighting illuminated the bridge. He could see fallen support beams, dangling sparking wires, and wounded crew everywhere. He stood, extended and curled his claws in a defiant gesture, just as reactor containment failed, turning his ship into a brief nova.

Commetriez did not have time to savor his victory. Two Krieg cruisers attacked T1911 from both sides. His vessel sustained several damaging hits before both of the Krieg warships were floating hulks without power signatures.

His satisfaction at the destruction of the enemy

cruisers was short lived. Two Krieg battleships closed in to avenge the obliteration of their commander's warship. T1911 was half again larger than each of the Krieg's vessels. However, the enemy weapons were firing from both sides at once.

The three battleships exchanged broadsides for several minutes. The sustained laser bursts brought down the shields and caused numerous hull breaches and partial loss of power in all three warships. The heavier weapons on T1911 caused more substantial damage. Suddenly, with secondary explosions throughout the Krieg warships, in quick succession, both of the battleships reactors lost containment and exploded. Commetriez was telling his chief engineers that he needed his shields restored when the violent concussion struck T1911 a devastating blow. It loosened Commetriez's command chair from its platform and bounced it off the wall. Extreme pain, then darkness descended over him.

Regaining consciousness and unbuckling his

seatbelt, Commetriez fell off his chair onto the floor. Blurry eyed, confused, and concussed, he looked across his bridge. Everywhere he looked, consoles were damaged, power was flickering in and out, and most of the bridge crew were either dead or mortally wounded. The abandon ship klaxon was blaring its message.

With blood streaming down his forehead and wondering what was happening, he staggered over to and pulled the dead communications officer from his chair. He called engineering and began listening to the damage reports. Incredulous that the Supreme Commander was still alive, the surviving engineering officer indicated that he had been unable to contact the bridge for the past twenty minutes.

T1911 was mortally wounded and was being protected by other fleet vessels. The engineer had shut down four of the reactors, and the fifth was nearing containment breach. He was frantically attempting to shut it down, but most of the power conduits connecting to it were severed. Up to this point, the engineer thought he was the most senior officer still alive, and as long as he remained at his station, he could possibly reroute power to the containment barrier. He also informed Commetriez that the bridge deck was cut off and that the only means of evacuation was the escape pods. A frigate was alongside and was retrieving survivors.

Commetriez 's initial intention was to go down with his ship. He was persuaded by the engineer and the frigate's captain that as the battle was continuing Commetriez should switch his flag as the frigate. Reluctantly realizing that both of his colleagues were correct, Commetriez looked around the bridge for additional survivors. Two of the other officers were still alive and mobile. Together they helped each other stagger down the corridor to the escape pod and evacuated his dying vessel.

Seeing the bridge escape pod, the frigate redirected a shuttle to retrieve the survivors. Once on the bridge of the frigate, Commetriez reasserted control of his fleet. As the frigate moved away from T1911, the last reactor lost containment, and the mighty warship disappeared in a nuclear explosion.

The tide of battle had turned against the defenders. The Krieg had lost thirty-five of their dreadnaughts, with another fifteen so damaged significantly enough to be effectively out of action. However, only ten defender battleships remained, five of them substantially damaged.

Several Krieg battleships were slugging it out against the defense platforms and the ground-based lasers. As they watched, one more Krieg dreadnaught exploded. Two others simultaneously targeted that battle station, which fired back. Minutes later it also erupted in a titanic explosion. More alarming, another dozen new Krieg battleships were entering the system through the captured portal.

The flank attacks on the Krieg resulted in them failing to close the envelopment. That failure left the central portal leading to the Home

System open. Commetriez ordered his surviving vessels to break off the engagement and escape through the gateway. His frigate was the last to leave.

Before transiting, Commetriez videoed General Akramaguian.

"Rigaloggo, I apologize for needing to retreat, leaving you to face the enemy alone. I must do so to save what is left of our fleet. However, I intend to return with a relief force."

Akramaguian replied, "Piercley, I am so glad to hear that you are alive. We all thought you were dead. You did all you could, and more than was expected. Your fleet destroyed over sixty percent of the Krieg fleet. We are taking down some more and will give them a hot reception when they attempt their landing. I have already initiated the self-destruct modes on the fleet and civilian shipyards. The Krieg will not be able to use our facilities for repairs."

As he was speaking, four Krieg cruisers docked at the shipyards to take possession. As the

Kriegster warriors rushed to enter the facilities, the chain reaction of explosions occurred. The shipyards disintegrated with sections crashing into the Krieg's vessels, with others spinning off into space or beginning their long fall into the atmosphere. The damaged Krieg warships began an uncontrolled spin into the atmosphere and destruction. With a cynical laugh, Akramaguian continued.

"Well, I could not have asked for better timing! We will still be here killing the Krieg when you bring the relief forces. Never fear, we will meet again and savor our ultimate victory."

Commetriez replied, "Until the next time my friend, and I will bring the drinks. Commetriez out." Then his frigate entered the portal.

Watching the frigate disappear on the scanners Akramaguian commented, "Well, now we are all that is left between our freedom and the Krieg. Let's destroy as many of them as we can while they are in orbit, then kill the rest when they land. Victory or death."

Chapter 20

Commander Trulegy Netscomb, leading his relief task force received a signal from one of the scout squadrons. The convoy of survivors from the Triberbrow system was straggling towards the Home System. The initial reports from the survivors were grim. The battle for the portal was lost, and the advancing Krieg dreadnaughts outnumbered Commetriez's battleships by more than two to one. Trulegy ordered them to make all possible speed towards Home, particularly the unfinished battleships which were assigned to the fleet repair yards.

Three days later, Commetriez retreating with the remnant of his fleet, appeared on Trulegy's scanners. Previously, he switched his flag to the largest active battleship T1731 and ordered the rest of the fleet to make all possible repairs. The Krieg would soon be following. He knew that Home's fleet facilities could repair his warships in a matter of weeks. The only question was did they have that much time.

Triberbrow Prime

After destroying the last of the defense platforms, the Krieg commanders issued a demand that the planet surrender unconditionally. When no answer was received, the Krieg brought up their troop transports.

Landing craft, each with a capacity of fifty warriors consisting of Krieg officers and Kriegster warriors began to deploy, and hundreds of them headed towards designated landing zones near major cities. Suddenly orbital space lit up with laser beams striking the transports, exploding inside the open launch bays incinerating all in the area. Several of the vessels exploded before the landers could be deployed. The others pulled back, to be out of range.

The landing craft did not fare any better. Lasers flashed among them destroying fifty percent in the upper atmosphere, resulting in them falling like shooting stars. Upon reaching lower altitudes, sprint style missiles tore them apart. Only ten percent made it to the designated coordinates, and the pride warriors were wiped out before they could establish any beachheads. The first wave was utterly destroyed.

The Krieg commander, not wanting a nuclear wasteland, ordered the warships to begin a two-day orbital bombardment with conventional weapons. Anticipating this, General Akramaguian moved his soldiers into prepared bomb shelters. The lasers and kinetic weapons, targeting identified defensive positions, laid waste to the countryside. The cities were spared, as the Krieg wanted the infrastructure for their own colonists. He then issued another unconditional surrender ultimatum.

When his demands went unanswered, the Alpha Male ordered another orbital bombardment, while his transports loaded the warriors into the landing craft at a safer distance from the planet. This time the landing zones were on the outskirts of the cities. As the landers approached the upper atmosphere, the ground-based lasers flashed among them picking them off like hanging fruit.

The landing craft nearing planetside were ravaged by the missiles. Krieg warships bombarded the areas surrounding the landing zones to hinder the defending troops. Twenty-five percent of the attackers reached the coordinates and came under heavy ground fire. Minutes later defensive missiles rained down upon the Krieg breaking up the warrior concentrations into small groups trying to get into the cities. The defenders mounted counterattacks, with concentrated laser fire which overwhelmed the warrior's personal shields, and wiped out the remaining warriors.

Frustrated, the Krieg Alpha Males challenged the commander's authority. After a series of individual combats to determine the final challenger, the commander was slain in single battle. The new prime alpha male ripped out his opponent's heart, while he still lived, and feasted on it to gain the other's strength. The victor then killed the dead opponent's cubs and mated with the female consorts.

Refreshed, the next day he ordered a combined kinetic and nuclear bombardment of the cities using neutron weapons. As the first bombs landed, blast doors shut cutting off the subterranean sections of the cities. The impact of the kinetic weapons ripped open some of the upper underground levels. The collapsing structures and penetrating neutron radiation killed thousands, mostly civilians as the soldiers battle armor provided a measure of protection.

The third wave immediately followed the bombardment, landing in demolished areas of the cities. Finally, the Krieg began to establish beachheads which sustained heavy fire from soldiers hunkered down in the rubble, which provided highly defensible positions. More landing craft arrived, and dozens were shot down with shoulder-launched missiles. The reinforced Kriegster warriors began to expand the landing zones. Vicious house to house and street to street fighting erupted with no quarter asked or given.

The warriors searched for access points to the subterranean sections. At every intersection, they encountered booby traps and heavy defensive fire. Casualties began to be excessive. The Krieg armies were finally able to land battle tanks which started to roam the countryside. Landmines and shoulder-launched missiles devastated the armored columns. The orbital fleet maintained a bombardment of identified defender positions. Fleet units venturing too close were struck by the land-based lasers. The assault bogged down into a battle of attrition.

Chapter 21

Home System

Supreme Commander Minion greeted Commetriez as his flagship docked at the naval repair facility. The hospital shuttles were removing the wounded and transporting them to hospitals on the planet. Work crews were already facilitating repairs of the damages.

The four previously uncompleted Triberbrow battleships were almost ready for their shakedown cruises. Currently, the four battlewagons were mated by construction airlocks at the end of the docking spine. The battle damaged dreadnaughts already were being moved by tugs into the vacated repair docks.

Commetriez handed Minion a digital copy of the battle report and then asked, "When can we mount a relief force? General Akramaguian and the military can hold out for months. However, the civilian population, particularly those in the subterranean cities are in great danger."

Minion replied, "First, we need to determine the strength of the Krieg. Triberbrow and Home were equally defended. However, with no fault directed to you, Triberbrow was overrun in a matter of days. The same thing could happen here.

"We need to wait for the report from the scouting missions to fully evaluate the situation. As it stands, the addition of your fourteen battleships and support vessels may be all that stands between us and extinction. Let's take the shuttle to my command center where we can thoroughly analyze this situation."

Soon after arriving at the command center Minion received an urgent message that unknown warships were entering from a seldom-used portal, the one in the directions provided the Earth people. Minutes later a drone's communication reached them providing the IFF recognition transponder information of the transiting fleet. Those matched the transponder information supplied by the Earth's Admiral Shepard.

Minion looked at Commetriez and said, "Assistance may have arrived. You approved of my initiative to our long-lost children. It seems they have sent a fleet of sorts to formalize our reunion. I have a prepared welcome message for this Admiral Shepard. Please review it and advise me if that is the correct approach."

USSP Texas

To the call of Admiral on the Bridge, Admiral Shepard and the Secretary of Defense Robert Treat walked onto the bridge to the greeting of his flag Captain, Robert L. Gibson.

Gibson informed, "Admiral and Mr. Secretary, we are approaching the gate to Upsilon Andromedea. Admiral, please take the command chair and lead us through at this historic moment of the first contact."

Shepard smiled and stated, "Captain, the chair is yours. Fly your ship into our meeting with our forefathers."

Gibson sat down and ordered Lt. Garvey, "Helmsman, launch the drone, then take us through."

Five minutes after emerging into the Upsilon Andromedea the communications officer stated, "Admiral, Sir, we just received a message for you."

Shepard replied, "Thank you, Ensign, I will take it in my ready room."

With that, Admiral Shepard and Robert Treat left the bridge. While seated at his private console, he opened the message.

Our greetings to you, Admiral Shepard and your Earth allies. We welcome you to what you call Andromeda 4, and we call Home. Our joy to greet you is tempered by the fact that war is at our borders. Our nearest allied planetary system has fallen to the Krieg. We are now caring for their survivors and refugees. I invite you and your allies to a conference at my command center. The coordinates are attached. Please bring your warships into orbit around our planet orbiting the fourth gas giant in the system.

Garand Minion, Supreme Commander.

Shephard and Treat read the message twice. Both exhaled deeply looking at each other. Treat spoke first.

"If true, this means if the Krieg wins here, they are only two weeks from Earth. Who knows, maybe quicker if they know of different portals. We need to stop them and drive them back from here. We need reinforcements."

Shepard agreed and added, I will set up a conference with our allies. To paraphrase, we can fight together now, or hang separately."

Together, Robert and the Admiral composed a brief message to Supreme Commanded Minion indicating that his signal was received, and they would certainly meet with him at his command center.

As the last warships transited, Shepard requested an urgent conference call with the fleet admirals. One by one they answered and the meeting was scheduled in two hours.

Home Command Center

Minion and Commetriez read the return message, then Minion said, "Well, at least they did not turn around and leave. I hope that means they realize the threat to their home system and are willing to coordinate with us."

Commetriez agreed, and then opined, "You indicated they represent a divided planet. Some of them may elect to fight, while others decide to return to their home. Sensors indicate they have twelve battleship class warships plus many cruisers. We need that firepower."

Minion added, "Very true, but do they have the type of weaponry which can kill the Krieg vessels? We will soon find out."

Admiral Shepard read Garand Minion's welcome message to the fleet admirals. He then opined, "We knew that we could be entering a war zone, but we did not anticipate we could be under imminent attack. I have discussed this with the Secretary of Defense, and he agrees. We will stay and fight. The rest of you need to make your own decisions. In five to six hours we will be entering orbit. It is yours to consider. However, I will need your answers before then."

Prince Hitachi immediately spoke up. "I am an heir in the line of succession to the Chrysanthemum Throne. I speak for my brother and father." Then with great emphasis, he stated: "My answer is *Bushido*. We follow the path of the Samurai, the Way of the Warrior."

Admiral Scheer then spoke, "I can't say it any better than that. We all knew this could be a fight. Let us get it done."

Sir William Stavely was very concise, stating, "Hear, Hear."

In quick succession, the French, Italian and Liberian, Brazilian, Indian, and Hellene admirals also quickly agreed.

Admiral Shepard then stated, "Thank you, gentlemen. I had no doubt of your commitment to this endeavor. It is so important to demonstrate that we are united against a common enemy. I will arrange for the meeting with Supreme Commander Minion as soon as we reach a stable orbit. Shepard out."

Chapter 22

Home System - Command Center

A procession of twelve shuttles from the Earth fleet flew into the large landing bay. Officers who were trained to speak in the representative languages greeted each party and brought them to the Officers' Club dining area for the social reception.

Minion, Commetriez, and the High Commissioners of Home and Triberbrow stood and greeted the delegations from Earth as they entered. The major-domo announced them with their title and rank as they strode in. Robert Treet was wearing a navy blue pin-stripe three-piece suit. Admiral Shepard wore his Full Naval Dress White uniform with his four stars on the shoulder boards. Prince Hitachi wore a Samurai uniform with his Katana and Wakizashi in lacquered wooden scabbards hung from his waist. The other officers wore their full military dress uniforms.

The most notable difference between the Andromeda people and the Earth representatives was the height. Most of the Andromedan males were over seven feet tall, the women over six feet tall, and both were of slender build. The Earth males averaged six feet tall, the women five-foot-seven, and both were of a much more substantial build.

Both groups mixed freely as the Andromedans were trained in the various Earth languages spoken. It was soon apparent that English was spoken by all from Earth, and most conversations were then held using that. Finally, the reception ended, and the attendees filed into two separate conference rooms, one for the military and the other for the civilian leaders.

The Earth admirals entered the conference room which was managed by Supreme Commanders Minion and Commetriez. Minion commented, "Thank you all for answering our request and arriving at such a dire moment.

The Krieg are at what you term our doorstep, having just recently captured the Triberbrow System. Rest assured, the fighting still continues on Triberbrow Prime, but without relief, the defenders shall inevitably fall. The Home System is the last inhabited bastion between your occupied space and the Krieg. If it were to fall, your systems would be next.

"The Krieg have advanced weaponry, such as our own. For generations, the war was a stalemate. It is only in the recent past that they have possessed a method of quickly replacing destroyed and repairing damaged warships deep within our systems. Previously, their incursions ended when we were able to slow them down, and cut their long supply lines. Then we would drive them back until war weariness caused the politicians to seek a peace agreement, which would last for maybe a generation. That assessment is no longer valid, as they are moving fast with an almost unending supply of battleships.

"Your fleet is very welcome in this conflict.

However, for your own sake, we offer to test your weaponry on our shields, and ours against your ablative armor. This can be done by us installing shielding on one of our asteroids, and you test your weapons. We could then do the same for a test of your ablative armor against our energy weapons. That way maybe we could provide improvements for each other."

Admiral Shepard answered, "You are welcome to tour our battleships and inspect our weaponry. We welcome the testing, as no one wants to go into battle unprepared. If you would, please tell us what happened during the fighting in and around the Triberbrow System. You are familiar with our history. We are very adept at warfare. Unfortunately, up until this time it has been against each other. Now there is a common enemy which needs to be removed. We may have some unique tactics which will assist in our mutual goal."

Commetriez walked to the podium and began to relate the battle for the Triberbrow System starting with the gateway battle, the effectiveness of the minefields, the ship to ship engagements and the gradual retreat leading to the invasion of the planet. The Earth officers were busy taking notes. When he finished, Admiral Scheer stood and asked, "You mentioned nuclear weapons. Are these the same created from nuclear fission which leaves a radioactive residue lasting thousands of years"?

Commetriez answered, "We only used these weapons in space where the fallout quickly dissipates. They are useful in destroying or disabling an enemy vessel. The upside is the missile does not have to actually hit the enemies warship. An explosion, within what you call a kilometer causes substantial damage to the vessel, and irradiates the crew. Three to five of those near explosions will kill the ship. Of course, one direct hit in the proper place will do the same.

"In our darkest history, we used them while attacking planets. Thirty-thousand of your years ago, it became a war of annihilation. Both the Krieg and we made hundreds of planets uninhabitable. It is our understanding that you recently discovered and are inhabiting one of them. There are others in your near space, maybe you have found them, also. We are ashamed of our past. That is why our politicians sought peace when victory was at hand. We did not want to reach that tipping point."

Scheer emphasized stating: "We discovered and experimented with them also, before realizing that we could destroy ourselves with them. We banned them for planetary use. However, each of our warships has a supply of the warheads which can be mounted on top of missiles. Thank you for providing the targeting zone and the required amount of ordinance."

Sir William Stavely then stood up and asked, "You did not mention the use of smaller fighter/bombers to attack the enemy while their point defense is engaging incoming missiles. My question - is it that you do not have them, or that you did and found them not to be useful?"

Minion and Commetriez looked at each other

with a puzzled expression. Minion requested, "Please describe this type of weapon, and how can such a small vessel as you call a fighter/bomber be able to damage a battleship?"

Sir William answered, "We call these warbirds. The fighter version has only the pilot and has wing and fuselage mounted lasers, plus the capacity of two missiles, which can be either used for aerial combat or be nuclear equipped to attack larger warships. They are small and fast. If an enemy has its own fighters, our warbirds go in first to engage them.

"The bomber version is more substantial, slightly slower, with a pilot, a navigator, and a weapons officer. Once our fighters engage the enemy, the bombers go in to attack the big ships. The pilot flies the warbird, the navigator, uses the computer to create the most evasive course, and the weapons officer will deploy counter-measures and release the weapons, including four missiles capable of nuclear warheads. This could be a big advantage in the war. It would seem that if you don't have these craft, the Krieg probably don't, either."

Minion and Commetriez looked at each other thoughtfully. Then Minion spoke up, "Could we have a demonstration of this type of attack on a fully armed battleship using the defensive lasers at the lowest power"?

Admiral Shepard answered, "By all means. Our flight crews have been practicing these same maneuvers to keep them and our point defense sharp during our journey. The rules of engagement are as follows:

1. The warbirds will come in waves to test the point defense weapons all across your battleships.
2. If your point defense is locked on to the warbird, it is considered to be shot down.
3. If fighter or bomber reaches firing range, then evades, the missile is determined to be a hit, as in real time

the impact would be mere seconds away.
4. For the point of the exercise, the firing range is one-thousand kilometers for a fighter, fifteen-hundred for the slower and less maneuverable bombers.
5. The attackers will do multiple evasive maneuvers during the assault to evade point defense fire.
6. Four or more hits on an unshielded battleship will determine it to be destroyed.

The eyes of Minion and Commetriez lit up. Commetriez exclaimed, "An actual battle simulation utilizing trained warriors in combat, facing an entirely new threat scenario. What a capital idea to test the skills of our personnel versus your pilots. I for one eagerly anticipate the results. How quickly can we get this done?"

Shepard answered, "We can conduct the exercise tomorrow. Send me the schematics of your shielding strength and what you know of the stability of the Krieg shields. We will use that to determine whether to use kiloton or megaton simulated weapons. We can jointly program our computers to the simulator mode to calculate damage from each hit. How many of your battleships do you want to enter the exercise? That will determine how many squadrons I will commit."

Minion and Commetriez decided on five.

Shepard replied, "Excellent, we will deploy three squadrons, each containing twenty-four warbirds. Each of them will be divided up into four flights of six aircraft. The pilots will be representing all of our allies."

Dates were also set for the testing of Andromedan and Earth warship and personal armor shields using spare parts on a deserted asteroid.

The civilian diplomats met in the adjacent conference room. Robert Treat, the spokesperson for the Earth diplomats, worked in conjunction with them to craft a cooperative agreement with the Home and Triberbrow High

Commissioners. In essence, the deal created full diplomatic relations between the Earth nations and the planetary governments of the Home and Triberbrow Systems.

A Mutual defense treaty was crafted to deal with the current crisis. Future negotiations would promote a more permanent solution. Draft documents were created. A second meeting was scheduled in two days to allow for mutually acceptable additions and deletions. The official signing ceremony would take place on the third day.

An official state dinner took place after the meetings. The officers and diplomats mixed freely, with friendships forged from the negotiations. Much of the conversation focused on the next day's war games and the unknown quality of the Earth fleet's weapons and tactics. The gala ended with high expectations from both sides.

Chapter 23

Admiral Shepard held a video conference with the fleet commanders and the Commander of the Air Groups (CAGS). He said, "It is time to break out the scorecards of our practice during the journey. I want our best seventy-two crews to man the warbirds. We don't know the exact quality of their point defense standards, but likely they are trained to bring down incoming missiles, not highly trained and skilled pilots. This will be our first demonstration of what we can do. However we have prepared for this, and I am confident of our success.

"Colonel Dan Burns's, the CAG of *USSP Texas* will lead the Alpha Squadron as his pilots compiled the overall highest score. He will get the first pick out of the top fighter and bomber crews. The next CAG in line is Colonel Heinrich Kohl from *SMS Bismark*. He will get the second picks. The third CAG is Francis Dieppe, representing the *Richelieu* who will pick third. Gentlemen, make a game of it and select your best teams. Make your own rules and trade pilots if needed. Have them ready by 08:00 tomorrow morning."

That night, flight crews throughout the fleet watched on live television as their members were drafted into the various squadrons. Good natured cheering and insults passed through the message boards, particularly when the last flight crew was selected.

The next morning, the five combined Home and Triberbrow battleships formed up in a line of battle. The warbirds formed up in their squadrons and began their attack runs.

Colonel Burns's squadron had the honors to lead the first run. Alpha Flight leader Captain Kent Fogtman, the top scoring fighter pilot, led his two wingmen against the first battleship. The point defense laser fire was intense. The pilots jinked their warbirds erratically up and down, and side to side evading the laser beams. At fifteen-hundred kilometers away from warship the bay doors opened and the inverted

'V' bracket, which would hold missiles descended. At one-thousand klicks, the three warbirds launched, then split in wildly evasive maneuvers flying directly over the battleship, which was maneuvering to evade. The scorers registered four hits, reducing the shielding capacity by fifty percent.

The second flight, bombers led by Lt. Jeffrey Kauffman, followed close behind, also making wild evasive moves. At two-thousand kilometers, they also prepared to launch. The right wingman, Igor Klotsky's warbird, was locked on and determined to be destroyed. Two of the six missiles were direct hits, one missed, and the fourth struck a glancing blow. Those hits reduced the shields to twenty percent, and point defense by thirty percent.

Colonel Burns led the third flight into much-reduced point defense fire, with all three warbirds launching at one-thousand klicks. Three missiles made direct hits, one hit the bottom side, and two missed. The result took down the shields and caused two hull breaches.

The fourth flight, bombers led by Lt. Connor Williamson launched at fifteen-thousand kilometers, with five hits. The battleship was considered to be destroyed and left the line. Colonel Burns squadron returned to *USS Texas* for simulated rearming.

At the Command Center, Commanders Minion and Commetriez looked at each other with disbelief. A battleship destroyed so quickly while taking down only one attacking warbird. A feeling of dread descended as Colonel Kohl's squadron continued their runs. So far, two of the flights had attacked with five hits reducing the shields down to thirty percent, while losing two warbirds.

The third battleship also came under attack. The second run was in process, with two hits registered and one warbird shot down. More unbelievable, Colonel Burns squadron began to emerge from the launch bays after a fifteen-minute turnaround. Before alpha leader could get into position to attack the fourth battleship Minion contacted Shepard to call off the exercise. The point was made. Three battleships destroyed, with only six of the attackers shot down.

Minion asked, "How do we obtain warbirds of our own, and how long does it take for a pilot to be qualified to fly."

Shepard answered: "I will provide you with the schematic diagrams for our warbirds and the flight simulators to train your pilots. You will have to make adjustments to the cockpits to accommodate your pilots. Your engineers and officers can also visit my battlewagon and her sister ships to learn about the launch bay operations. I will also make arrangements for flight instructors to assist your pilot trainees."

The next day the testing on the ablative warship armor occurred. It was suddenly apparent that the stronger Andromedan lasers could penetrate into the battleships with concentrated fire. To correct this, Minion shared the Andromedan shielding technology. Quickly, the Earth vessels entered the shipyards for installation of shield generating emitters.

The Andromedan engineers also reprogrammed the fusion reactors to spread the load for the power needed to create and maintain the shields. Within two weeks, the modifications were installed.

During the same time, it was determined that, although the Earth soldiers' laser weapons would not penetrate Krieg personal shielding, the handheld fusion powered railgun assault weapons shredded the Krieg shields. More deadly was the Motorized Squad Automatic Railguns (MSAR), which utilized a three-soldier crew on a fusion-powered motorized carriage. An ablative armor shield offered protection for the operators and the gun. Those heavy kinetic weapons could penetrate a bunker or decimate the attacking enemy ground troops.

The Andromedan officers were fascinated by the railgun technology. While high-energy laser battlefield weapons took enormous power to operate and were difficult to maintain, a portable fusion battery, kept inside the stock of the assault gun, made the deadly weapon inexpensive to produce and maintain. The MSAR operated on a battery weighing less than two-hundred pounds enclosed in an ablative armored case, bolted to the carriage. Arrangements were made for an exchange of technology and weaponry.

Shepard sent drones back to Delta Pavonis, relaying the success of the alliance and the new technology for enhanced shields and more powerful lasers. He also requested reinforcements once the shield modifications were installed on the existing warships.

Chapter 24

Commander Trulegy Netscomb's scouts retrieved a stealth drone as it returned from the Triberbrow System. The robot contained a message, relayed from a second stealth drone returning from the system beyond Triberbrow. After viewing the news, he transmitted it to his Supreme Commander Minion.

The news was ominous. The Krieg were repairing thirty of their damaged battleships in a portable shipyard, now positioned behind the gate leading from the vacant system to Triberbrow. Large factory ships were mining asteroids to manufacture parts and components for the repairs to the damaged warships.

Triberbrow itself was garrisoned by fifty Krieg battleships, and the Krieg were mining the asteroids to fabricate sections to rebuild the shipyards. The conflict continued on the planet itself. Intercepted communications indicated that the Krieg subdued almost thirty percent of the land mass, and were being hotly contested in the rest. A tight beam laser message to General Akramaguian informed him that unknown allies joined the Andromedans and relief was imminent.

The gathered intelligence indicated the Krieg were probably not aware of the other two portals, as the drones did not pick up any traffic in and out. This confirmed the Andromedan theory, as the scouts and picket ships on the Andromeda side did not detect any Krieg warships.

Once relayed to Minion and Commetriez, they both decided to bring Admiral Shepard and his newly enhanced fleet up to date. The relief force to Triberbrow was now or never. Shepard agreed, as did his commanders. However, with the concurrence of his fleet, Shepard had a side plan.

While the united home and Triberbrow fleets consisting of eighty-four battleships, attacked through the central gate, the Earth fleet would strike through the second gateway, closest to the captured gate, make a transit through that gate and destroy the ships under repair, the factory ships, and the portable shipyard.

Following revisions, the plan was approved. The two fleets powered away to conduct a coordinated attack. Both fleets completed their transit through the portal into the empty system. Minion and Commetriez's fleet joined with Commander Trulegy's task force and continued on following the middle path towards Triberbrow.

The Earth fleet used the secondary portal pathway to enter towards the end of the Triberbrow System to transit in on the flank. If the coordination were correct, the Earth fleet would complete their entrance one-hour after the battle began, which would draw the available Krieg warships into the initial engagement.

A courier delivered the probe's message to

General Akramaguian. He was puzzled as to who the new allies might be, but that was irrelevant to his situation. He was in his backup command center, as the original was discovered, then captured by suicide squads of Kriegsters. When the attackers reached the command center's blast doors, he ordered the tunnels detonated, crushing the Kriegsters under tons of rock. His command staff exited the headquarters through secondary tunnels which were then collapsed.

The battle on the surface was as expected. The Krieg had the personnel and held the high orbitals. The Krieg eventually broke into the subterranean shelters under the cities. The brutal house to house fighting in the different inhabited levels resulted in the Krieg taking enormous casualties. When they finally won those battles, the captives were brutalized before being brought into the detention centers.

Akramaguian's rapid response teams used a honeycomb of tunnels to ambush Kriegster units on the surface with small arms and anti-tank weapons. The Krieg responded quickly with orbital bombardment. It was a war of attrition, and his defenders were slowly losing.

Akramaguian had one ace left to play. In the Krieg-occupied territory, four ground-based lasers, located in concealed caves, had a clear shot at the reconstructed space dock. His defenders could possibly hold out for another month before his supplies, and almost exhausted men were gone. His last effort would be to destroy it before it became operational.

Chapter 25

Second Battle of Triberbrow

The long-expected Andromedan attack began with scout ships and frigates pouring through the central gateway. The minefields blocked entry to the smaller vessels, which fired their lasers into the mines to clear a path, losing seven warships. The light and heavy cruisers followed next, widening the breach, with five of them destroyed or damaged. With the pathway cleared, the battleships transited.

The Krieg sent a tight beam laser message to the picket ships at their entrance portal for reinforcements, then positioned their battleships and cruisers to block the Andromedans. It would take several hours for the battle to begin.

Admiral Shepard took the precaution of transiting his scouts and frigates first. As expected, no minefield was present. The first ships sent a drone back that the way was clear, and that twenty Krieg battleships, ten cruisers, and thirty frigates had transited through the captured gateway.

Shepard ordered all flight crews into their warbirds as the capital ships entered the portal. One by one as they emerged, the warbirds launched and formed up in squadrons under their CAGs.

The Alpha Male leading the Krieg reinforcements looked at the computer analysis of the Earth warships as they emerged from the gate.

Contemptuously he muttered, "What is this, puny battleships and cruisers of an unknown type trying to obstruct our great advance? What, look, swarms of gnats emerging from them. We will swat them like flies, then join our brother prides in this great conquest. Let us attack before they can organize. Launch missiles."

Over one thousand of them headed towards the Earth Fleet.

Colonel Burns wirelessed his colleagues, Colonel Tom Quelly and Colonel David Evans, the CAGs of *USSP California* and *USSP New York* as their combined strike force of 300 warbirds checked in with their squadron and flight leaders. Two-hundred of them were fighters, equipped with two missiles with five megaton warheads. The one-hundred bombers carried four rockets with ten-megaton warheads.

Burns stated, "Keep the formations loose to allow for evasive maneuvers on the bomb runs. This will be our first engagement up against live fire. Our pilots need to maintain their focus, even when their wingmates are shot down. As soon as the bombs are released, the warbirds are to return to base for refuel and rearm. The second and third runs will be disorganized. Single pilots and bomber crews are to join up with others to make their second or third runs. Good luck and Good Hunting!"

The other wing commanders gave similar

speeches. Over four-hundred warbirds comprised of the French, Italians, Hellenes, Liberians, Brazilians, and the Australians launched the first wave, attacking the escorts. The second and third waves included the Americans, Japanese, Austro-Germans and the British with a combined eight-hundred and fifty warbirds flew over the first wave, focusing on the battleships.

The CAGs hung back directing their squadron commanders and flight leaders. The fighter pilots and bomber crews flew through the point defense fire to deliver the loads. Several five-megaton explosions usually took down the escorts shields leaving them open to direct hits on the hull. The com traffic was heavy with pilots exulting over a direct hit, or the destruction of a Krieg warship. Others were the panicked cries of the crews as their warbirds were hit and spun out of control. Other icons just disappeared from a direct hit.

Following the first wave attacks, fifteen Krieg frigates and ten cruisers were either destroyed or were drifting hulks without power. Several others sustained hull breaches, with crews desperately attempting to make repairs.

The Earth warships suffered under the missile onslaught. The interceptor missiles, counter-measures, and point defense destroyed 95% of the attackers. Near miss, explosions destroyed two cruisers and three frigates and damaged *LMS Liberia*, the *Richelieu*, *USSP California*, and *SMS Bismark*. Thanks to the Andromedan shields, all of the damaged warships remained operational while damage control crews scrambled to make the needed repairs.

The warbirds sustained ten percent casualties with two or three percent of the crews ejecting and floating in their escape capsules. Their only hope was for their locator beacons to be found before their air supply expired.

The surviving warbirds flew back to the red light lit landing bays with their thrusters pushing back to slow them enough so the tail hooks could pull them to a stop. Several warbirds were damaged, crashing in the retrieval bay. Automatic extinguishers put out the fires, and tugs with plows pushed the wreckage off to the side to keep the landing area clear. Medical crews then attempted to rescue any surviving crew members.

Conveyors grabbed the nose gear and pulled each warbird into the supply area, where the pit crews worked rapidly to refuel and rearm the craft. The canopies rose, and flight attendants climbed the ladders to give the pilots food and water. Within fifteen minutes the conveyors moved the warbird onto the catapults, which launched them back into the battle.

Chapter 26

Commetriez's flag flew on the new Triberbrow battleship T2110. It was a super dreadnaught, over twice the size of the largest Earth warships. Minion's flag flew on H35617, the most modern and largest Home warship. By mutual agreement, the Triberbrow squadron took the lead, with Commetriez commanding the fifth battleship in line.

The Andromedan and Krieg battleships launched thousands of multi-megaton nuclear missiles against each other. Both navies then launched interceptor missiles and deployed countermeasures.

The interceptor missiles did not have to hit, which was almost impossible due to the closing velocity speeds. Each had a one-megaton warhead which exploded in proximity. The force of the explosion often detonated the offensive warhead or scrambled the guidance system causing it to miss the target.

On average, eighty percent of the attacking missiles were destroyed or took erratic courses. The point defense consisting of lasers and kinetic shotgun bursts targeted the survivors. The battleships also took erratic maneuvers to evade as required. The butcher's bill from the missile attacks tallied eight Andromedan and seven Krieg battleships destroyed or disabled.

Commetriez's battlewagon sustained two near misses on the port side reducing shielding by fifty percent. The engineers rerouted power through other conduits to balance the load which restored the shields. Minion's battleship came through the onslaught undamaged.

Both navies then formed up into opposing lines of battle. The slugfest was about to begin. The Krieg Alpha commander remained confident, as he knew reinforcements were on the way. The reinforcement's Alpha leader assured him that the unknown fleet of smaller warships would quickly be swept aside.

Colonels Burns, Quelly, and Evans directed their squadrons in their attack runs towards the five leading Krieg battleships. The Austro-Germans, British and the Japanese picked out their own targets. The slower two-hundred bombers trailed the attack with instructions to assault damaged battlewagons of opportunity.

The fighters bore in braving the defensive fire, jinking wildly and firing lasers to confuse the Krieg targeting systems. At fifteen hundred kilometers, the Krieg battleship fuselages filled the windshield. The bomb bay doors opened, and the pilots pushed the firing stud, pulling back on the controls to avoid a collision. Some of the more inexperienced did not make it.

One by one the Krieg battleships began to drop out of line. The bombers then pounced. The Krieg Alpha Male could not believe what was happening. Who were these madmen who closed rapidly in little ships to deploy their missiles? His battleship was struck four times and only had partial, flickering shields, with many hull breaches.

Lt. Yoichi Haikaido piloted his bomber at the Alpha Male's battleship, flying through the point defense fire. Suddenly a laser clipped his wing causing the craft to spin. While Yoichi was fighting to regain control, the warbird rapidly approached the battleship. Realizing there was no possible escape he piloted the bomber along the length the battlewagon, lasers destroying defensive weapons and shield emitters. Finally, the shields dropped. Grinning, he yelled there and aimed for one of the hull breaches. The crew shouted BANZAI as they entered the opening while the weapons officer manually detonated all four of the missiles. The Krieg battleship disintegrated in a nuclear fireball.

Prince Hitachi, standing in the *Yamato's* command center was watching and listening to the battle communications from his warbirds. One, a bomber flying next to a battleship drew his attention. Listening to their conversation, he saw the bomber's icon merge with the battlewagon, followed by a titanic explosion. He grunted, "Bushido."

The attacks petered out, and the surviving warbirds returned to their bases. The attack destroyed ten of the Krieg battleships with two others severely damaged and out of the battle line. Again the butcher's bill was high. Eighty-eight of the warbirds did not return. Search, and rescue shuttles launched homing in on the escape pod beacons. Thirty-seven flight crew members were brought back to their mother craft.

Through the chaos of the landing bays, Colonels Burns and Quelly led their squadrons on the next run. Colonel Evans, in a damaged fighter, made a hard emergency landing. The medics lifted him out of his cockpit with bruised or broken ribs, bleeding heavily from the head, and a likely concussion. Orderlies took him to sickbay. Captain Kent Fogtman, was given a brevet promotion to Major and appointed as the temporary wing commander of the *USSP New York*.

Near Triberbrow Prime the slugfest continued.

The weight of numbers was against the Krieg warriors, who were losing the engagement. Already, one-half of his battleships were destroyed or so damaged to be useless.

The Alpha Commander looked with dismay as swarms of small ships decimated his reinforcements. Their commander, aboard a severely damaged battleship, reported that the small vessels carried nuclear missiles and launched them at close range before attempting an escape. Suddenly, that battlewagon's icon disappeared. The surviving reinforcements were in disarray and scattered, while another swarm approached them.

Commetriez was elated. The battle was going well. The Krieg were being decimated, and he now had a two to one advantage in battleships. The addition of Admiral Shepard's fleet was a spectacular success. There would be no Krieg reinforcements. Their main battle fleet, while still dangerous, was doomed, with no avenues of escape. He would not be content until they were utterly destroyed.

Minion contacted Commetriez and suggested the Home fleet could finish off the remaining Krieg battleships. Go to your planet, relieve the ground forces, and rescue your citizens. Commetriez agreed, and his remaining fleet changed course for Triberbrew Prime.

As he reached high orbit, he contacted Akramaguian's headquarters, announcing his return. The general replied, "Our sensors detected the space battle, so you must have won."

Commetriez replied, "I am sorry it took us so long, and I am so relieved that you are still alive. As for the battle, Supreme Commander Minnion's Home Fleet is mopping up. When our transports make orbit, we will send down the soldiers. Don't shoot them down." Chuckling, Akramaguian said, "No worries, we don't have any missiles left. Who are these allies, and what role do they play in this battle?"

Commetriez said, "They are our long lost descendants, from a planet they call Earth.

They have occupied the systems around their planet. Their fleet is in the process of destroying the Krieg reinforcements. They have revolutionary tactics in space combat. They also have provided us with very interesting and useful ground assault weaponry. You will meet them soon."

The rearmed warbirds descended onto the Krieg warships. The flights formed up in rows against the Krieg's vessels, attacking relentlessly. The pilots followed the previous attack, launching missiles until the Krieg warship was destroyed. The Krieg fought back bravely, and none attempted to escape. Space combat is unforgiving. In two hours, it was over, with no Krieg survivors. The cost was high, another forty-one warbirds were shot down.

Shepard's fleet retrieved the warbirds, while search and rescue shuttles looked for and picked up the ejected crews. Then the fleet formed up and headed towards the gateway to transit into the Krieg occupied system.

The pilots exited their planes and headed for the showers and a hot meal. Some also headed for their racks and tried to sleep. Others gathered in the Pilots' Club to exchange stories. All were now combated veterans. They toasted the dead and congratulated each other. All too soon they would be back in their warbirds, waiting to be catapulted into the next fight.

Chapter 27

Shepard's fleet emerged from the gateway with shields up and the pilots in the warbird cockpits. Once all the systems came back up, the sensors clearly illustrated the extent of the Krieg shipbuilding and repair facilities. A dozen battleships were moored to the docks, many appearing to be in the final stages of completion. A dozen patrolling frigates and light cruisers provided protection for the facility.

Shepard ordered the launching of all the warbirds and a missile strike of the facilities and the escorts. The launch tubes rose from their storage facilities, flushed the racks and descended to be reloaded. The warbirds followed closely behind the third salvo.

Krieg interceptor missiles rose up, took down seventy percent of the first salvo, fifty percent of the second. And less than ten percent of the third. The facility was not heavily defended, as it was in a vacant system in a pacified territory.

The missiles struck the shipyards and factory ships a devasting blow. Four of the battleships were destroyed and five substantially damaged. Three of the battlewagons disengaged the moorings and began to power up to engage.

The cruisers and frigates suffered severely. Only five of them survived, all of them damaged. Minutes later, the warbirds swept in to make their attack runs. Duplicating the tactics of the previous battle, they formed up in flights against the battleships, the surviving cruisers, frigates, and factory ships, relentlessly hammering them with the nuclear-warhead tipped torpedoes until all were destroyed.

Shepard sent a probe back through the gateway with a message to Minion that the mission succeeded. He also dispatched a stealth drone into the next system to determine its status.

The next day, the warbirds surveyed all the asteroids showing signs of mining. Those with airlocks received special attention. Marines, equipped with breach boxes and handheld rail guns landed to search the tunnels. After breaching the airlock wall, flash-bang grenades were tossed in. Following a brief firefight, the guards were killed. Moving deeper into the mines, the soldiers discovered human slaves, naked except for scraps of clothing, working in sub-human conditions.

Shuttles were called in, docked at the *USSP Texas* landing bays. Shepard ordered the terrified captives be housed in an emptied munitions warehouse. The medics created a quarantined sickbay to provide care for the malnourished former slaves. Throughout the day, more shuttles arrived with captives suffering a similar plight. Shepard sent another drone back to Triberbrow notifying Commetriez of the slaves.

With the space battle over, the Andromeda warships focused on the elimination of the last pockets of Krieg resistance in the asteroids. The transport ships, escorted by frigates, transited into the system and entered orbit over Triberbrow Prime. Landing craft delivered tens of thousands of troops. The mass-produced MSAR's were first introduced into actual combat.

The Krieg soldiers' personal shields were totally ineffective. The kinetic rounds also destroyed their defensive positions. The Andromedan soldiers then moved in to mop up. Many of them were equipped with the new handheld railguns, which assisted them in overrunning Kreig positions.

General Akramaguian's troops emerged from their tunnels, attacking the Kreigster soldiers from behind. Caught between the hammer and the anvil the Kreig officers encouraged their soldiers to conduct suicide attacks. Eventually, the Kriegsters survival instincts took over. Discontent grew in the ranks. Tired of being ordered into the slaughter, they revolted, turned their weapons on their officers, then surrendered.

The internment camps were emptied. Krieg scientists had begun the process of inserting implants into captives considered worthy to be soldiers. The technicians were initially coerced, then willingly reversed the process. Being scientists, they deplored the practice. However, they followed orders as the Krieg were a militaristic society, ruled by a military elite.

Some of the captive Kriegster soldiers also volunteered to be deprogrammed. Not all the implants could be removed, as they integrated with the body's systems, altering the DNA.

The technicians were able to isolate the mind control implants and neutralized them. To test the neutralization, a scientist dressed up as a Krieg officer, barking out commands. He barely escaped the room as the deprogrammed soldiers first resisted the controls, then tried to kill him.

The deprogrammed soldiers went back to their comrades, who had already shown evidence they could be deprogrammed by disobeying orders when they revolted against their officers. Observing the change in the programmed soldiers, the others willingly agreed to the process.

However, there was a significant problem. The male and female Kriegsters could reproduce, and the children had the same physical characteristics as their parents. The mind control was a program implemented after they reached puberty and were removed from their parents. The Andromedan society would not tolerate a Kriegster presence in the community.

The Andromedans placed the almost completed shipyard into immediate use. The debris from the space battle was gathered by sweepers and fed into the fabricators to manufacture replacement parts. The asteroids, towed by the Krieg to be near the docks, were ground up for the same purposes. That allowed the damaged warships to be brought to the shipyard for repairs and rearming. The fleet quickly began to regain its strength.

Chapter 28

The stealth drone returned two days later with ominous news. The surveyed system was a duplicate of the one Shepard just pacified. Thirty Krieg battleships were under construction at the shipyards, several nearly complete. Like the current one, it appeared to be lightly defended. Not wanting to get ahead of his supply line, Shepard decided to hold his ground and sent a probe back to Triberbrow requesting reinforcements. He also rotated the warbird squadrons to provide a continuous combat space patrol to alert of any Krieg incursions.

Receiving Shepard's message, Minion now knew how the Krieg were continually resupplied with new ships and equipment. Gathering forty battleships and fifty escorts, he departed Triberbrow Prime to join Shepard. Minion also brought an empty troop transport to bring the former slaves back to Triberbrow. On the second day, he transited the portal to join up with Shepard's fleet.

Minion invited Shepard to an informal dinner with him on H35617. Shepard's shuttle docked, and he was immediately taken to Minion's ready room. There, before the stewards arrived with the meal, they talked strategy.

First, Minion brought Shepard up to speed about the destruction of the Krieg fleet at Triberbrow Prime, and the reduction of their ground forces. Shepard was particularly interested in the plight of the deprogrammed Kriegsters.

He commented, "If I understand you correctly, the Kriegsters are now a sub-species of humanity. To create their warriors, the Krieg altered their human DNA with the implants, which cannot be removed. Because of that, and their history of being tools of the Krieg, they and their children are unlikely to ever be accepted in Andromedan society."

Minion agreed.

Shepard then indicated, "I have an idea which may resolve this issue. First I have to talk to the Secretary of Defense."

Minion thought about that and then stated, "I am intrigued. However, it is not something that has to be fixed today. There are more important things at hand, such as what to do about the Krieg repair facilities in the next system."

He then spread out star maps, pointing to the gateways on either side of their current system, and the next containing the Krieg facilities. He then highlighted an asteroid field located in both systems opposite each other; even though they were separated by several light years.

Minion stated, "Old trader stories, handed down over generations tell of a smuggler's route through the asteroids. In our past time of internal troubles, with systems competing with and often fighting each other, traders avoided high taxes on both sides by smuggling. Much of the inter-system commerce passed through the smugglers, who avoided the customs checkpoints at the gateways. I suspect that there is a smuggler's portal through those asteroids. I have sent a stealth drone to find out. If it transits and returns, we will know for sure.

"When my fleet transits through the gateway, it will attract all their attention. Your navy could escort my assault ships as they move undetected through the asteroid field portal and come up behind the facility. The warbirds can take out the static defenses which will allow my troops to land and take the shipyards intact. We could possibly even capture some of the Krieg battleships.

"If worse comes to worst, your warships can still destroy the shipyard and the unfinished battleships while they are still docked. My fleet can deal with the other Krieg warships and the factory ships. "

Shepard agreed with the plan and stated, "If the portal exists, the enemy can be hit from both sides at the same time. If it is a myth, then the combined fleets will transit the gateway together and destroy the Krieg facilities and warships."

The next two days were spent checking the other asteroids for inhabited mines. Three were discovered, and the miners were liberated. On the third day, the stealth probe returned. The smuggler portal existed and was large enough to accommodate Shepard's fleet. Additional information included that ten of the battleships were complete and moored adjacent to the shipyards. It was unknown if they were battle-ready and had crews aboard.

The next day, Shepard's fleet and the assault ships set course for the smugglers portal. Two cruisers and three frigates were left on patrol duty, while the Andromedan fleet headed directly for the gateway to the Krieg-occupied system.

Shepard's fleet transited with full shields deployed. Asteroids from both systems accompanied them on the trip through the gateway. Emerging from the other side, Shepard ordered the first wave of pilots into their warbirds, while the other waves waited in the ready rooms. The magnetic aura from the asteroids blocked sensor readings. As the battleships cleared the asteroids, the first wave of fighters launched off the catapults.

The battle between the Andromedan fleet and the Krieg was fully engaged. Over the past two days, Krieg reinforcements of twenty additional battleships had arrived. Coupled with the ten new Krieg battleships, and five others releasing their docking clamps, the odds were almost even between the two fleets.

Major Kent Fogtman led the first wave of warbirds as they swept in undetected out of the dense asteroid field. Dozens of torpedoes armed with five-megaton warheads smashed into the five Krieg battleships while they were still attempting to clear the shipyard. One by one, they exploded in nuclear fireballs. The concussions rocked the shipyard, with sections breaking off. Three incomplete battlewagons, still attached to shipyard sections began to drift away. Shepard, seeing the shipyard breaking apart contacted the assault ships with new orders.

"The shipyard capture is a no go. New targets, capture those floating Krieg battleships before they can destroy them. My cruisers will escort you in and suppress enemy fire as needed. Shepard out."

Fogtman led the warbirds which had discharged their torpedos on a strafing run of the shipyard, destroying the fixed laser emplacements. Several Krieg shuttles launched in an attempt to reach the floating battleships. Fogtman's fighters shot them all down, then provided cover as the assault ships dispatched shuttles full of soldiers to capture the targeted warships.

With the loss of five battleships for their battle line, the Krieg were now outnumbered. The two battle lines slugged it out firing lasers at point blank range. Overloaded shields on both sides failed. Hull breaches caused wounded battlewagons to fall out of the battle line. Shepard's bombers, seeking targets of opportunity pounced on the damaged Krieg warships, destroying them with multiple hits from well-placed ten-megaton torpedoes.

Aboard H35617, Minion was grimly satisfied with the direction of the battle. While sustaining moderate damage, his battleship's shields were still holding at twenty-five percent. His fleet had lost five battlewagons to ten Krieg, three of those thanks to Shepard's bombers taking out the damaged warships.

The weight of his battleline was now overwhelming, and the outcome of the battle already decided. The only item to be determined was the butcher's bill. He watched on his screen as three of the bombers approached in line abreast towards the Krieg battleship which H35617 had just knocked out of the line. Simultaneously, each of the warbirds launched two torpedos then broke off. The bomber passing above the battlewagon was struck by the point defense and spun out of control. The command capsule ejected. Seconds later internal explosions shook the battleship which became a fireball, consuming the expelled crew.

The Andromedan soldiers, using multiple breach boxes assaulted the three floating Krieg battleships from several entry points. The Kriegster soldiers defended vigorously. The kinetic projectiles from the assault crew's handheld rail guns cut through the Kriegsters personal shields and swept them away. The soldiers rushed to the engineering departments and the bridge decks to cut power to the self-destruct systems.

The brave attempts failed. Even with the power cut, the countdowns continued. The soldiers rushed to the escape pods, and several other teams reboarded their shuttles. As the assault teams vectored away, the Krieg battleships exploded. The search and rescue shuttles pulled the survivors to safety.

Not wanting to risk any more personnel,

Shepard ordered the other incomplete battleships and the remnants of the shipyard destroyed by the warbirds. Lining up by flight, the fighters and bombers made their pass launching their torpedos until nothing but debris remained.

Chapter 29

Hours later, Minion and Shepard discussed the after action reports in Shepard's ready room on *USSP Texas*.

Minion began, "Always remember, a battle plan seldom survives the first engagement. You fleet performed magnificently. First, the attempt to capture the Krieg battleships. When their self-destruct systems prevented that possibility, you destroyed their entire facility. The Krieg reinforcements were not anticipated. Your warbirds destroyed the five just operational battleships before they could become a factor. That changed the metrics of the battle.

"Your bombers also destroyed all the Krieg battlewagons which dropped out of the line of battle. That is very important, as often, given time, a damaged battleship can return to the engagement with devastating results. Your bombers never gave them the opportunity to make repairs. That allowed the weight of our broadsides to destroy the Krieg battle line.

"This war may be the last one we fight with a reliance on a navy's battle line. Your warbirds have changed everything. All our future construction will utilize the methods of war you have introduced. Our current advantage is that none of the Krieg who witnessed the recent battles are known to have survived. We need to press that advantage while it still exists."

Shepard replied, "Thank you for the compliments on our fleet's performance. However, we were just following the brilliant plan you devised. Finding the back-door into their system was genius, which allowed us to trap them in a pincer attack. You designed the strategy, we just assisted in its implementation.

"Don't discard the line of battle strategy so quickly. Your navy was brought up with it, and attitudes are difficult to change. Real change takes time to adapt. Our version of the battleship will not be able to stand up in a line of battle. They are very versatile but are not equivalent to your massive warships. My suggestion is to employ both concepts, and develop tactics for them to support each other.

"I suggest our next move is to survey the next system to determine if the Krieg are utilizing it similarly. Do you know of a back-door we can employ to observe incognito? The smugglers might have used another connective pathway for their operations. The Krieg, being recent conquerors, are unlikely to know of the locations."

Projecting star maps on Shepard's screen, Minion outlined a similar path between this and the next station.

He reminded, "These all are uninhabitable brown dwarf star systems, useful only as pathways between inhabitable systems, and the natural resources contained within each. Other than means for collecting toll revenues, they were largely ignored. As valuable as the rare minerals are, inhabited planets have asteroids much closer and more economical to exploit.

"The smugglers, on the other hand, found them as a desirable means for exploitation, and a way around paying tolls. While the powerful systems ignored the opportunity, the individuals explored, exploited, and discovered the hidden portals. It is just a matter of knowing where to look, and a willingness to take the risk."

Highlighting on the electronic map, Minnion continued, "The common factors are asteroid fields located on similar planes of a void. There is likely somewhere within the void a pathway for the asteroids to follow. One just needs to take the time to find it and have a reason for doing so."

With a wry smile, Minion continued, "As a confession, my family has a rich history of one of the most prominent merchant barons in the sector. It is rumored, that they, on occasion, dabbled in smuggling. I uncovered these maps while searching the archives in the family library. It is only this war that brought them to importance."

Shepard chuckled, and then said, "I suspected as much. You need to talk to the Secretary of Defense about his family history. It also is fascinating."

Minion replied, "Given the opportunity, I will do just that. In the meantime, I have already sent two stealth drones, one through the main gateway, and the other to search for the smuggler's path. I suspect it is there, and I believe I know where it is. With both of them, we have the opportunity to gain new information. If the Krieg positions are there, possibly we can utilize the same strategy as we did in the last battle."

Nodding, Shepard then said, "Speaking of new knowledge, did you ever determine the origin of the human slaves in the mines? We were not able to communicate with them. They seemed to have an entirely different dialect, and were as terrified of us as they were of the Krieg."

Minion replied, "They are not from this sector. Initial testing indicates that it is possible they are of same genetic stock as the original

Kriegsters. From DNA samples, the technicians have theorized they are distant ancestors from the dispersal following the first Krieg wars. Our colonists scattered, as their worlds were made uninhabitable in the nuclear holocausts. Once the Krieg recovered, these people could have been near the beginning of their conquests. Now that they were discovered, we will do our best to rehabilitate them."

Two days later, both drones returned. The smuggler's path was almost identical to the previous one. The Krieg were there, but they were in the process of dismantling the shipyard and towing the sections away while they evacuated the system. It was possible they were over-extended, and the recent losses of over one-hundred battleships ended their current expansion operations.

The allies were left with two choices. Allow the Kreig forces to depart, or pursue and destroy them while they retreated. The Earth admirals met with Minion in his ready room on H35617. All the options were discussed.

Minion opined, "We have the opportunity to destroy these Krieg forces and end the war. Too many times in the past, they were allowed to withdraw, only to return when they regained their strength. However, my forces are not adequate to complete this objective. I will need your assistance."

Looking around the gathered officers, he continued, "You all have fought bravely, far away from your own territory. Your assistance has turned the tide. I will understand if you want to return to your own systems."

Shepard spoke up, "The job is unfinished. The United States will stay."

Admiral Scheer. Prince Hitachi, and Sir William Stavely also quickly agreed. The Australians supported Sir William.

Admiral Horace Taylor of Liberia stated, "Where the United States goes, we go with them."

Admiral Francois Picard from France and Admiral Guiseppe Mareno from Italy demurred. Picard spoke for both of them.

"Supreme commander Minion, we were glad to assist you to drive back the Krieg menace. However, we feel it is time we went home. We will bring first-hand reports of this struggle, and the progress being made.

"You provided us with significant enhancements for our warships, including the new shield technology. The medical advances your physicians provide will be most valuable to our population. Admiral Marino and I agree that we need to take this information back to Earth."

Then looking at his fellow admirals, he said, "Please provide us with your dispatches directed towards your diplomatic personnel. We will, of course, bring any of them who wish to return to Earth with us."

The Brazilian and Indian commanders agreed with Picard and Mareno. They considered the mission completed. It was time to go home.

Minion was gratified at the continued support of most of the allied fleet. He thanked the departing admirals for their much-needed support. As the allied shuttles departed, he sent drones to Home and Triberbrow advising them of the Krieg retreat, his pursuit, and request additional warships.

The next morning, the departing allies began their transits to the Home System. There they delivered dispatches and picked up the departing diplomats. Secretary of Defense Treat opted to remain at the Home System but released his staff to return. He read Shepard's message, then prepared two sets of documents. One he placed in the diplomatic pouch presented to his deputy, and the other, with a personal letter to Emily, in an Andromedan drone directed to Delta Pavonis. He was sure those messages would be delivered to Earth before the departing fleet arrived.

Chapter 30

The next three days were spent mopping up Krieg mining asteroids and liberating more of the slaves. On the fourth day, Commetriez aboard his flagship battleship T2110, five other warships from Triberbrow, and twenty battlewagons from Home arrived, providing Minion his reinforcements. Thirty cruisers and frigates also came as escorts.

Scout ships transited the gateway and found the next system empty. The fleet transited and set full speed for the next portal. The faster scout trips transited the smuggler's gateways to determine the Krieg positions. Again they discovered the Krieg continued their retreat and transited through the primary gate to deliver the news.

The Pursuit continued until the fifth transit into the home system of the former Regalian Empire. Their, the Krieg were suppressing an uprising by the conquered population. The

Krieg warships included twenty battleships, thirty cruisers, and twenty-three frigates. Three transport ships were in orbit around Regal Prime.

As the allied fleet transited, the Krieg warships broke orbit and formed up to meet them. With the line of battle engagement three hours away, the Earth warships launched their fighters and bombers. Three waves of five-hundred warbirds advanced ahead of the battle line which fired its missiles high over the pilots at the developing Krieg battle line.

Following close behind the nuclear strikes, the waves separated into squadrons, then into flights. Major Fogtman directed his wing against two damaged battleships, with the columns of flights launching their nuclear warhead torpedos. Colonels Burns, Quelly and Heinrich Kohl did the same. The British and Japanese bombers followed. When the last of the warbird waves broke off to rearm, only ten Krieg battleships, fourteen cruisers, and eleven frigates remained. Forty-five warbirds were shot down in the engagements.

Minion arranged his battleships into two lines, which would pass on either side of the surviving Krieg. The one-sided engagement ended quickly with the destruction of the Krieg battle line with only minor damage to the Andromeda battlewagons.

The rearmed warbirds took off in hot pursuit of the cruisers, frigates and the three transport ships which retrieved the Kriegsters on the planet. Two hours later the fighters and bombers returned with the report that none of the Krieg ships escaped. Another ten warbirds had fallen. The search and rescue shuttles retrieved eleven ejected pilots and three bomber crews.

While the Earth warships retrieved their warbirds, the Andromedans began to enter the orbit of Regulus Prime. The orbital scanners indicated a planet devastated by bombardment from the Krieg warships. Minion ordered the Marines stationed on the battleships to board the landing craft and begin to drop to the surfaces. The Marine patrols encountered stunned survivors starting to emerge from the rubble. With the infrastructure of the planet destroyed, the best way to avoid starvation was an evacuation of the system. Minion sent a drone to Home to advise them of the crisis. Before leaving he provided the Marines with supplies for temporary housing and food for the survivors.

A search of the four other systems previously ruled by the Regalian Empire indicated a Krieg evacuation, leaving similar conditions as they departed. A Humanitarian crisis of unimaginable proportions confronted the Andromedans. As much as they desired to continue the pursuit of the Krieg, the more critical responsibility prevailed.

Scouting missions to the next several systems reported that a fleet of twenty Krieg Battleships and an unknown number of support warships passed through a few days previously, then disappeared. Minion ordered a sweep of the next five systems. After a week of searching, no traces developed. All the data indicated a complete Krieg evacuation. It became apparent that the war had ground to an end.

The combined fleets transited back into the Triberbrow system, where Commetriez and his warships stopped. Shepard saluted him in a conference call and declined an invitation to visit.

He said, "We are a long way from our homes, the war is over, and it is time we returned to our families. I look forward to our next meeting, hopefully under better circumstances."

Chapter 31

Emily read Robert's letter while recuperating in the hospital. She cried and smiled as he told her how much he loved and missed her. His return would be delayed only by a few months. The war was going well with the Krieg in full retreat. He talked about retirement after President Bush's term in office. It was well past time they spent their time together.

"Oh, Robert," she thought. We both know that it is not in you to retire."

The doctor just left her room with grim news. She had fallen off her horse and cracked two ribs. The X-rays revealed growths in both breasts. Further testing indicated she had stage 4 metastatic cancer in both breasts. The prognosis was that she if she underwent a double mastectomy her life-expectancy was one to three years, and six months or less if the surgery was not performed. Emily did not want to make this decision alone. However, this was not something one put in a letter.

Emily looked back on her full life. In college she was a top athlete, she married into a famous navy family, had three grown children with successful careers. She played an essential role while a planetary governor's wife and held two undersecretary positions in presidential cabinets. Robert was the love of her life, and her one and only lover. He deserved more than to return to a wife who was one-half a woman, with a short life expectancy. Robert mentioned the miracles of the Andromedan medical advancements. Just maybe she would live long enough to find out.

Emily reflected on her children who were married and off the planet. Robert IV was recently promoted to Captain. His cruiser *USSP De Moines* patrolled space between Delta Pavonis and Beta Hydri.

Anne lived on Mars. She had a highly paid position as the Customs Flight Tracking Administrator at the Mars Port passenger terminal. No vessels entered or left the port the port unless all the manifests and passenger lists passed her scrutiny.

Abigail was a Ph.D. of Archeology and lived with her family on Beta Hydri. She was responsible for one of the newer sites with promising discoveries.

Emily realized the decision was hers alone. When the surgeon and the oncologist visited, she told them no. The doctors reminded her of her life expectancy.

Emily replied, "If I only have six months to live, I will do it my way."

She checked herself out of the hospital and went back to work as Undersecretary of the Interior for Colonial Affairs. It was time to schedule a tour. One week later, Emily and three assistants departed with Mars as the first stop on their itinerary.
Her first stop was at Mars base. Following a day of official duties, she spent a wonderful evening with Anne and her three teenage

grandchildren Robert, 17, Beth, 15, and Annie, 13. They laughed about old memories and made plans for a family reunion when grandfather returned. The next day she and her staff boarded the Department of Interior cutter for the trip to Beta Hydri 4.

The planet had not changed from her last visit. Abigail's site was located in the tropical zone. Temperatures hovered between ninety-five to one-hundred and five degrees. Dressed in a light pair of shorts, work boots, and a loose blouse over sports bras, Emily joined Abigail and toured the site. As they approached a zone with residual radiation, Abigail stopped, saying that to go any further they needed protective clothing.

Emily shrugged. Suddenly, Abigail looked into her mother's eyes and said, "I feel something is terribly wrong with you. There is something different about your demeanor. Your indifference to the radiation danger indicates you are not telling me something. I need to know."

Smiling wistfully Emily replied, "I have stage four breast cancer, with six months or less to live. I am still strong enough to visit with my children and complete my duties. On this, my final trip, I am doing both."

Abigail asked, "Does father know"?

Emily replied, "No, I just learned myself. He is still in the Andromeda sector and won't be back for months. I will still be here when he returns. I received a letter from him via diplomatic pouch. The war is almost over with the Krieg in full retreat. Please keep all that I have said strictly confidential."

Abigail looked at her mother disapprovingly and then said, "Dad needs to know. I understand your refusal for the surgery. Given that choice, I would probably do the same. But you must tell him so he can decide when to come home."

Emily smiled, and then said, "We will see."

That night, Emily, Abigail, her husband Eric, and

son, Joseph, enjoyed a family dinner. Eric, also a Ph.D., was animated about the discoveries. Many artifacts from the ancients could have real application in current society. Emily smiled at his enthusiasm. He and Abigail were perfectly matched.

Joseph was accepted into Yale University and planned to major in archeology. His work at the Beta Hydri sites provided him needed experience, and would be applied to his internship. Emily congratulated him on his acceptance and told him she was proud of his accomplishments.

The next day was full of official duties with Emily and her staff visiting with local municipal authorities and the planetary governor. Her flight to Delta Pavonis was the next day.

Abigail, Eric, and Joseph flew in to dine with her at a local restaurant. Looking at Eric, Emily understood he knew. As they walked her back to the hotel, she held both of their hands. In the lobby, Abigail said, "Mom, remember what we discussed, please tell him."

Emily smiled brightly, kissed them all good-bye, and took the elevator to her room. That night she penned a personal and confidential letter to Robert. The message told him of the diagnosis, her refusal of the surgery, and her current trip. Emily also enclosed a digital copy of the medical report. She ended asking him to bring an Andromedan physician home and to come quickly.

The next morning she took the packet to the governor's office, asking him to prioritize the message to the Secretary of Defense at the Home System in the Andromeda sector. He placed it into the diplomatic pouch and assured her it would be dispatched by a drone that very day. Thanking him for his assistance, she joined the staff on the cutter which took off for Delta Pavonis 4.

Chapter 32

Washington, DC

President Bush held his regularly scheduled cabinet meeting. He asked Vice President William Davis to read The secretary of Defense's message on the progress of the Krieg War and the state of the alliance with the Andromedans. In his report, Robert stressed the mutual advantages derived.

The timely arrival of the Earth fleet with their warbird strategy turned the tide of the war. The provision of the rail gun technology gave the Andromedan soldiers a clear advantage over the Kreigsters.

In return, the Andromedans provided the shield technology, upgraded the reactor efficiency, and enhanced the power of the laser weaponry. Their advanced medical technology allowed the average Andromedan to live over two-hundred years. With the application of this technology, most of the diseases suffered by the Earth's population could be eliminated.

Bush handed the letter to the Under Secretary of Defense, Ronald Graves. He then asked, "What is the status of the installation of the shield emitters, the reactor upgrades, and the power enhancements for the laser?"

Graves replied, "All the warships in the Sol System have completed the upgrades. The squadrons in the colonial systems were recalled for the installation and are being replaced by a similar number of completed task forces. The transition of the warships should be finished today."

Bush then asked the Secretary of the Interior Donald Hodel of the latest news from the colonies. Hodel replied, "Mr. President, the Under-Secretary, Emily Treat left last week on her tour. So far she has visited Mars and Beta Hydri 4 and submitted her reports by courier. "There is nothing unusual to report, just suggestions for some minor changes in procedures. She and her staff are now en route to Delta Pavonis 4. Emily is a hands-on investigator. If anything is in need of discovery, she will find it."

Bush asked the Secretary of Human Services Otis Bowen the status of the new Andromedan medical technologies. Otis replied, "Mr. President, the data was turned over to the FDA. There is a panel reviewing the technology. Hopefully, a 'Black Hole' won't occur, as the FDA is notoriously slow in releasing anything new. When I reviewed the data, it looked promising. I will do everything to expedite the review."

Satisfied with the progress, Bush ended the meeting.

Delta Pavonis System

The Department of Interior cutter transited through the gateway and headed at full speed to Delta Pavonis 4. Emily and her staff were reviewing their itinerary when the RED ALERT warning sounded.

A scout ship, commanded by Lt. Jack Holmes, searching the edge of the system full of asteroids noted unusual activity, partially masked by the electromagnetic interference of the asteroids. With the sensors set on a broadband scan, Holmes proceeded cautiously.

Minutes later a portal opened, and a fleet of unknown warships began pouring through. Undetected due to the interference by the asteroids, Holmes shadowed the fleet. Within an hour, the sensors confirmed a fleet of twenty Krieg battleships, thirty support warships, and two transport ships were on a direct course for Delta Pavonis 4. Holmes launched two drones on different paths. Both broadcast the emergency message upon exiting the asteroid field.

The cutter transporting Emily and her staff had passed the point of no return when the emergency message broadcast. The Krieg warships would intercept them if they tried to turn around and escape through the gateway.

The pilot wirelessed their situation to the Delta Pavonis Command Center indicating they were traveling at full speed and would arrive two days before the Krieg.

Chapter 33

On Delta Pavonis 4, the base commander, Rear Admiral Benjamin Halleck, commanded eight battleships, *USSP Ohio, USSP Virginia, USSP Vermont, USSP Kansas, USSP Maryland, USSP Puerto Rico, USSP Cuba*, and *USSP Alaska*. Additional warships included ten cruisers and fourteen frigates. All of them recently completed the weaponry and shield emitter upgrades.

Fortunately, all were in the system for the training sessions involving the shield technology, and the upgraded laser. Halleck canceled all leaves and ordered the crews back to their warships.

Halleck also commanded fifty-four warbird squadrons including forty- eight assigned to the fleet. That armada was backed up by the three each based to the defense platforms. Seventy-five percent of those were fighters, the others were bombers.

The planetary defense, commanded by Major General Oscar Griswald, consisted of two-hundred warbirds, including one-hundred and fifty fighters, and fifty bombers. The air wings and their ground support crews were led by his second in command Brigadier General John Callahan.

The army units included three brigades of infantry and two armored which were equipped with M1A1 Abrams tanks. The infantry units weaponry interspaced M-16 automatic rifles, handheld rail guns, and MSARs. The two defense platforms were each defended by an artillery battalion to fire the laser weapons and launch the missiles.

Halleck's main concern was that many of the pilots were recent graduates from the Naval and Air Force Academy flight schools. None of the pilots had combat experience, particularly against enormous battleships protected by shields. The Pentagon sent most experienced pilots, and the larger nuclear warheads went to

Andromeda with Admiral Shepard.

His warbird pilots could utilize five-hundred Kiloton and one megaton warheads. That would mean that his inexperienced pilots would need to register a dozen or more focused hits on a Krieg battleship to bring down the shields, then several more to finally destroy it.

Later that day the cutter containing Emily and her staff touched down at the spaceport in Armstrong City. They were immediately brought into a meeting with Governor Jason Brown. She dismissed his concerns for her and the staff's safety. Her team would monitor activity at the public shelters. Emily asked for immediate transportation to the Dragon Academy. After all, she had developed the training curriculum for the dragons and the riders. Who was better qualified to oversee that operation. The governor began to protest about her safety. Emily gave him a practiced admiral's wife's stare. After a few moments, he backed down and called his aide to make the arrangements.

Washington DC

President Bush ordered the Red Alert to all the Earth-occupied systems, then he met with Casper Weinberger, Ronald Graves, and the Joint Chiefs of Staff. The military generals and admirals advised against a prompt relief fleet. The size of the Krieg fleet looked to be bait for a trap to ambush the relieving force.

With that in mind, Ronald Graves rejected Halleck's request for reinforcements. He explained that it was unknown if the current attack was a prelude for a general offensive against the Sol system and the other colonial systems.

Bush ordered Weinberger to meet with the space-faring nations' foreign ministers to determine their response. Initial phone conversations indicated that the Austro-Germans, Japanese, the British, French, and Italians would defend Earth from their defense platforms. However, their colonial forces would remain in place at least initially to protect their systems.

Captain Michael Smith, the garrison commander at Beta Hydri 4, received an urgent message from Ronald Graves recalling Admiral Shepard's fleet. Smith immediately dispatched a drone to the Home System in the Andromeda sector. In the best case scenario, the fleet would take at least ten days to return.

Chapter 34

Battle of Delta Pavonis

Admiral Halleck transferred his flag from the Command Center to *USSP Ohio*. His fleet was located one million miles from the planet and prepared to launch one thousand warbirds at the Krieg fleet. For the past thirty-six hours, his pilots had practiced on simulators the tactics developed by Admiral Shepard.

The lack of experience showed as less than ten percent of the fighter pilots, and bomber crews were able to escape their simulated attack runs from one-thousand and fifteen hundred kilometers, crashing into the Krieg warships. When the target range was extended from one-thousand klicks to three thousand for fighters, and from fifteen hundred to forty-five hundred for bombers, the survival rates were much improved. The drawback was that the greater distance provided the Krieg warships time to maneuver to cause the incoming warheads to miss.

The fighter pilots launched first, formed up into waves and swept forward to confront the Krieg. The bombers followed, twenty-thousand miles behind the initial waves. Together, one-thousand one-hundred warbirds advanced towards the Krieg fleet. Fifty-four provided a combat space patrol covering the fleet.

The squadron leaders directed their pilots on their attack vectors. The fighters would go in first, eight flights of six warbirds for each Krieg battleship. Those attacks were hoped to bring down or significantly weaken the shields by overloading the emitters. Then the bombers would go in launching their four one-megaton warheads at the weakest points.

Halleck's warships also launched their missiles, flushing the external racks, which descended into the ship for reloading. Several waves of the rockets would approach the Krieg warships one minute before the warbirds arrived.

The Krieg launched their defensive and offensive missiles at Halleck's fleet, which replied with their own defensive rockets. The combat air patrol would try to shoot down surviving incoming warheads, then the point defense would take over.

The first waves of fighters swept over the Krieg escorts, focusing on the battleships, damaged by near misses and out of position as they frantically maneuvered to avoid the warheads. The flights bore in, juking to avoid point defense fire and launched their five-hundred kiloton warheads into the battleship shields, which flickered under the nuclear impacts. Then the second wave followed, destroying dozens of emitters. The bombers then struck in columns of four, launching their five, one megaton warheads.

Three Krieg battleships were destroyed and four others significantly damaged. Most of the rest sustained weakened shields with the destruction of hundreds of emitters The Krieg point defense fire destroyed or disabled ninety-three warbirds. The surviving fighters and bombers returned to the fleet to rearm. To avoid fires and explosions from crashing damaged warbirds, Halleck ordered the ship captains to land the whole ones first, rearm and refuel them for the second strike. The crews of the severely damaged fighters and bombers were ordered to eject and wait for the search and rescue shuttles.

The second wave, including the fifty-four combat space patrol warbirds, went in copying the tactics of the first. The added warbirds brought the strength of the attack almost equal to the first. The focus of the fighter pilots was the lesser damaged battleships. That allowed three squadrons to target each battlewagon. Flight after the flight went in launching their nuclear warheads against the shields. After the second wave, exploding emitters weakened the shields. On the third wave, the emitters on three battleships wavered, then failed.

The bombers swept in against the warships with the failed or failing shields. The four previously damaged battleships exploded in nuclear fireballs. Three others, with numerous hull breaches, dropped out of the battle line. Four others sustained extensive battle damage but were still in the fight.

The butcher's bill on pilots and crews was high. One-hundred and three of the warbirds failed to return. The survivors returned to the defense platforms and the ground airbases for refueling and armaments.

Halleck ordered a third strike at the rapidly closing Krieg warships. This wave consisted of the two-hundred warbirds stationed on Delta Pavonis 4 and the six squadrons from the defense platforms. The warbirds went after the cruisers and undamaged battleships.

Just before the warships reached the engagement zone, the warbirds swept in, pummeling the shields of the active Krieg vessels. Two of the damaged battleships and five of the cruisers were destroyed. Late arriving bombers attacked the three battlewagons with hull breaches until all were vaporized.

Hallack's fleet was now within range of the Krieg lasers. He ordered maximum thrust to close the distance. As the Krieg lasers hit his warships the shields flared but held. After several hits, emitters began to overload, resulting in the shield power reducing to thirty percent. More Krieg laser blasts punched through, causing hull breaches up and down his battle line.

Finally, the Krieg warships were within laser fire range which flared on the weakened Krieg shields. Minutes later the rail guns were in range. The kinetic projectiles ripped through Krieg shields, punching holes in the hulls. Five Krieg battleships and seven cruisers exploded.

Hallock, on *USSP Ohio 's* smoke-filled command center listened as emergency beacons and abandon ship messages came flooding in from his battle line. Suddenly, *USSP Virginia* disappeared off his battle screen. She was quickly followed by *USSP Vermont, USSP Kansas,* and *USSP Cuba.* USSP *Ohio* shook as several more laser hits took down her shields causing hull breaches. Her railguns fired back at her tormentor, shredding the remaining emitters, and punched through to engineering. The Krieg battleship lost containment, with the resulting nuclear fireball also consuming unprotected *USSP Ohio.*

A rearmed fourth wave of warbirds swept into the chaotic battlezone, torpedoing every Krieg warship which could be targeted. The space battle turned into a ship to ship melee, with the warbirds lending assistance wherever they could. With the destruction of *USSP Maryland, USSP Puerto Rico,* and *USSP Alaska* the space battle ended with the annihilation of Hallack's fleet.

The Krieg suffered almost as much. Only two battleships, five cruisers, and four frigates survived, all substantially damaged. The lead Alpha male declared their opponents to be worthy prey, and it would be his honor to exterminate them. He then told his remaining fleet to move away from the planet and the tormenting smaller craft. It was time to complete the needed repairs and develop a better strategy to combat the warbirds.

The next day, the lead engineer came back with a potential solution.

"We must use their own technology against them. The most severe damage to our warships came from their weapons firing projectiles. During a search of the Battlespace, we recovered several of those weapons. Respectfully, sir, please hear my idea."

Following the presentation, the Alpha male smiled and said, "Make it happen."

Chapter 35

Washington, DC

The drones stationed at the portals leading to Sol, Beta Hydri, and Eta Cassiopeiae A & B reported on the progress of the battle up to the destruction of Hallack's fleet. The encrypted messages were relayed to the fleet commanders in those systems and to the White House. Secretary of State Weinberger informed President Bush of the disaster and the imminent attack on Delta Pavonis 4. Bush agonized about his decision not to send the relief fleet.

Weinberger cautioned, "Mr. President, follow the advice of the Joint Chiefs and the cabinet. You should marshall the fleet and work with our allies. Together we can be ready to repel any other invasion. Delta Pavonis is strongly defended and can hold out until the situation surrounding a possible full-scale invasion clears itself up. The fact that the seriously depleted

Krieg warships are still there lends credence to the baited trap theory. If we send the fleet in to engage the remaining Krieg, we could lose them all."

Delta Pavonis 4

At his command center on Defense Platform Alpha, General Oscar Griswald watched the battlefield developments with dismay. The defense of Delta Pavonis was now up to the defense platforms and the remaining warbirds.

However, the supply of nuclear-tipped warheads for the torpedoes would be exhausted after the launching of five-hundred warbirds. Most of the nuclear warhead storage was on the battleships. The final two attacks from the platforms and ground-based warbirds drastically reduced the stocks maintained there. Griswald criticized himself for not insisting that Admiral Hallack store more on the planet.

After a moment Griswald discarded the self-criticism as unproductive. He needed to move his command center to the underground facility tunneled deep under the mountains 100 miles from Armstrong City. He also needed to disperse the warbirds into the prepared underground shelters. He wirelessed General Callahan to meet him at the new Command Center. Before leaving, he ordered all non-essential staff to be evacuated from the platforms to the planet. He then boarded a shuttle which transported him and his team to the hidden hangers cut into the side on the mountain.

The Dragon Compound

Emily walked through the pens of dragons who immediately recognized her voice and scent and crowded around to get attention. The guards nervously watched as the beasts congregated around her. Emily showed no concern or fear as she had brought them up from hatchlings. She cooed and clucked with them. Many of the guards swore she and the dragons were talking.

Emily then organized a meeting with the dragon

trainers and riders, who dressed in blue and white camo uniforms could blend into the sky. She began, "By now, you all are aware of the disastrous defeat of our naval forces. That means, for at least a while, we are on our own. It will take time for a relief force to be organized and arrive. It is only a matter of time before the Krieg controls the high orbitals. There are several things we must do to prepare.

First, we must camouflage this compound, so it blends in with the surrounding forest. I had that in mind when I ordered its construction to appear as regular rock formations. Netting can be extended across the top to complete the appearance.

Second, the dragons and riders must be familiar sights in the sky and not look like they are on patrol. Conduct random flight patterns as if the animals are scanning the ground for prey. I am confident that the Krieg already have probes examining our planet looking for military concentrations.

Third, when the Krieg land and they will, we must be ready to observe their movements and send back narrow beam messages to General Griswald's staff. You riders will also be provided with portable laser and railguns for self-defense and for the elimination of scouts or stragglers whenever it can be done without being observed.

Remember the basic commands you were provided to communicate with your mounts. They are quite intelligent and will follow your orders. We will be our stealth army, ever present, but so common as to be ignored by the enemy."

The handlers then paired the riders with their mounts. Following a short period of familiarization, the dragons rose majestically into the sky to begin phase one of the program. Emily walked out of the forest, and with binoculars tried to see the riders. Even though she knew where to look, it was difficult. Satisfied, she entered the training facility which to the untrained eye resembled natural rock formations.

Andromeda 4

The transit to the Home System lifted the spirits of the fleet. One stop to pick up the diplomats remained and then a trip back to the Sol System. Upon arrival, Shepard learned that Robert Treat left the previous day with a team of Andromedan physicians in a fast scout ship. Apparently, Emily had cancer, and the physicians were confident that she could be cured.

While the fleet was still in Andromeda, The drone with the recall order transited. Sighting the navy, it began to transmit to Shepard. Listening to the message Shepard forwarded it to the other fleet commanders and ordered rapid preparations for the return trip.

Upon hearing the message, Minion provided a faster route, using the smuggler paths which would lead directly to Delta Pavonis. The faster frigates and cruisers set the pace. The modifications to and the rebalancing of the reactors increased the battleships' speed by thirty percent. Combined with the shorter route, that would cut ten days off the return trip.

Chapter 36

On the fourth day after the space battle, the Krieg Alpha male ordered the attack on Delta Pavonis. His five cruisers and four frigates formed a crescent-shaped formation in front of the two battleships. During the previous days, the engineers swept the battlespace for metal particles, bringing them back to the warships to be ground up into small jagged particles. The escort ships were equipped with copies of the captured railguns with the metal particles for ammunition. The intent was to throw up a screen of small pieces of metal in front of the advancing warbirds.

Observing the approaching Krieg warships, Griswald launched the warbirds, with the first strike from the platforms followed up by the planet based craft. As the warbirds approached, the Krieg escort screen maneuvered perpendicular to the approaching swarm and fired their rail guns.

The scanners on the attacking warbirds began to pick up fuzzy images. Suddenly the leading fighters started to explode. Cries from the lead pilots echoed the same report. Small pieces of metal all around them as their warbirds began to explode or spiral out of control when they flew into the rapidly expanding wall of metal.

With fifty of his warbirds destroyed or disabled, Griswald sent the abort message to the trailing fighters and bombers. He ordered the laser batteries on the platforms to fire wide beams into the screen of metal particles. Space lit up with a massive fireworks display. Griswald then ordered the warbirds into a second assault, this time in an enveloping maneuver from all sides instead straight in. The lead elements would be armed with laser only, to cut a pathway for the warbirds with the nuclear warheads.

The Krieg escorts kept on firing their railguns at the approaching swarm. This time the metal particles were less efficient as the laser batteries, and the fire from the warbirds began to cut holes in the screen. Like avenging angels, the warbirds attacked the picket ships striking their shields repeatedly with nuclear-tipped weapons.

Eventually, the overloaded emitters failed, and the torpedoes began to hit on the hulls. Some pilots exulted as their projectiles struck, exploding inside the Krieg warships. Others cried out in dismay as their warbirds spun out of control or exploded after being hit. With the antiaircraft fire suppressed, the remaining two-hundred warbirds began their attack runs on the battleships.

To the pilots' and Griswald's dismay, the battlewagons also had railguns as point defense. Attacked from all sides at once, the Krieg railguns still took an extreme toll on the warbirds. Thirty percent were shot down, and the scattered nature of the attacks made coordination of nuclear torpedo hits difficult.

Relentlessly, the pilots pressed their attacks. Initially, the Krieg shields held up, but they eventually began to flicker. Concentrating on the weakest shielded sections, torpedoes began to strike the battleships. When the last of the warbirds broke off, each battlewagon was hit over twenty times with several hull breaches. However, without a follow-up nuclear strike, both Krieg battleships survived, along with one of the cruisers.

The Krieg warships withdrew for repairs, then with their more extensive lasers with a greater range, they began a twenty-four hours bombardment of the defense platforms. After three days, much of the platforms were reduced to rubble. The alpha male then summoned the two transport ships to exit the asteroid belt to join his battleships.

Realizing that attempting to maintain the platforms would only result in the deaths of the surviving crew, Griswald ordered the activation of the self-destruct devices on the reactor containment controls, and the platforms were abandoned. Thirty minutes later, the self-destructs took down the containment barriers, and both platforms disappeared in nuclear explosions. The high orbital positions of the platforms negated any EMP effect. Most of the remnants of the platforms burned up upon reentry into the atmosphere.

The Krieg warships then took up positions in high orbit and began a bombardment of the spaceport, government buildings, the tourist oceanic cruise line docks, and visible military facilities. That night troop landing craft began their entry into the atmosphere. Anti-aircraft missiles and lasers began to target the Krieg landing craft. The first wave of the assault was decimated. The orbital bombardment targeted the missile and laser sites.

As the surviving Krieg and Kriegster warriors established beachheads, they came under missile attack. The missile sites also immediately came under orbital assault. Fortunately, as on the other sites before them, shortly after launching their weapons, the missile crews moved along an underground rail system to another defensive location, detonating the tunnels behind them.

The Krieg troops moved into Armstrong City looking for essential documents and public shelters. However, all they found were vacant buildings and an empty subway system. The spaceport and cruise ship terminal were also deserted.

The Dragon Center

Emily observed the live-feeds as from high overhead the dragons and their riders continued their continuous erratic patrols watching the Krieg soldiers and the effectiveness of planned harassment attacks. Additional landers approached the beachheads. Suddenly, shoulder-launched surface to air missiles struck several of the landers, some exploded in the air, others made hard landings. Other missiles streaked in and hit them just as the rescue crews arrived. The attackers disappeared into several camouflaged manholes. The dragons observed the Krieg search efforts for patterns which could be exploited.

Eventually, the searchers found the camouflaged openings and carefully entered to search the tunnels. Upon receiving a signal from a dragon rider, the defenders exploded hidden bombs collapsing the passageways onto the Kreigster warriors. For the next week, the Krieg slowly expanded the landing zones making them safer from hostile fire.

Delta Pavonis Command Center

Generals Griswald and Callahan met to evaluate the effectiveness of the resistance. To date, the Krieg were unable to locate the civilian shelters or the military command center. Eventually, that would change. Casualties from the ground fighting amounted to twelve percent of the forces. Half of those were dead, the rest recovering in the underground hospitals. Ammunition was still plentiful. One big surprise was the coordination with the dragon force which provided outstanding reconnaissance. The big questions remained. Where were the relief forces? Could the attack on Delta Pavonis be part of a broader offensive?

Washington, DC

President Bush and Vice President William Davis convened the daily cabinet meeting. Bush listened to the daily briefing, then pounded his fist on the table. Everyone turned quickly to look at him as he began speaking, "I am sick and tired of this cautious approach. If the Krieg were here in strength, our patrols would have found them."

Looking at the Undersecretary of Defense Ronald Graves, he resumed, "Ronald, I want the fleet alerted. We move tomorrow to relieve Delta Pavonis 4. Admiral Young will command. His second will be Admiral Cernan."

Looking at Casper Weinberger, he said, "Casper, inform our allies of my decision. Request their assistance. It will be an asset if they come. What good are they if they won't?"

Later that day, Weinberger brought a message to Bush. Both the Austro-Germans and the

British would participate. Admiral Jung would lead the Austro-German fleet through the portal from Zeta Tucanae. The Royal Navy, under Admiral Hardgraves, will transit with us through the Delta Pavonis gateway.

Satisfied that action was at hand, Bush left the Oval Office for the residence. There he and his wife, Barbara, spent a quiet evening in the White House.

Chapter 37

Delta Pavonis

The allied fleets transited into the system in a pincer movement to trap the Krieg. As their sensors came back online, a sudden massive disturbance occurred from the direction of the portal which the Krieg had entered. Admiral Young's initial response was that it indeed was a trap, and called the fleet to battle stations.

As the fleets prepared for battle, the transponders revealed the new warships were Admiral Shepard's fleet, which burst out of the asteroids at a previously unknown speed towards Delta Pavonis 4. On his bridge was the Secretary of Defense Robert Treat, whose scout ship had joined the fleet.

Shepard wirelessed Young and Jung and learned the Admiral Hallack's fleet was destroyed, and of the likelihood that the Krieg were preparing a trap. Shepard replied that his allied fleet would soon initiate the braking thrusters to slow them down enough to engage the Krieg warships and relieve the defenders at Delta Pavonis 4. Young's navy could protect one of his flanks in case other Krieg warships were concealed in the system. Admiral Jung agreed with the strategy. If a Krieg fleet were hidden in the asteroids, it would be attacked from all sides.

Shepard then sent a laser message to General Griswald alerting him that relief was days away. Shepard advised Griswald to prepare a counter-offensive as soon as the Krieg warships were drawn away from the planet. Griswald cautioned Shepard on the Krieg's employment of rail-gun point defenses, which had decimated his warbirds. He advised Shepard to instruct his pilots to utilize the englobing attack strategy.

The Krieg Alpha male learned of the invasion by the allied fleets. He realized that there was no escape and that the final battle was only days away.   If he could not win, then he would torch the planet. His ground troops began a systematic pattern of wanton destruction, while his warships began a relentless bombardment of Armstrong City and all the smaller cities and towns, which were spared up to this time as they did not have military value.

The Dragon Complex

Alerted by the reconnaissance teams of the senseless destruction of the planet's surface, Emily informed Griswald that her dragon teams could coordinate with Griswald's troops to stop the devastation. Griswald agreed and set up ambushes based on the dragon teams intelligence reports.

The Kriegster soldiers began burning the crops, fruit trees, and the forests. Suddenly ambushes were sprung with defender soldiers using their handheld rail guns drove them off. As the Kriegsters retreated, the dragon teams swooped down attacking from the rear. If the rider were shot down, the riderless dragon would swoop into the battle, pick up stragglers high into the air, then drop them.

Realizing that the dragons were actual combatants, the Krieg combat aircraft began to shoot them down. General Callahan ordered his warbirds to engage the Krieg aircraft. The air above the battle zones was filled with dog fighting airplanes. With so many planes involved, the Krieg warships could not intervene without killing their own pilots. Gradually, the warbird pilots, better tactically trained to fight in trios, gained the upper hand in the air battles.

Orbit

The Krieg Alpha male observed the approach of Shepards fleet and left orbit to intercept. He considered that the fully repaired battlewagons were more than a match for the human's smaller battleships. The troop transports were converted into railgun ships to deal with the hated warbirds. He knew that eventually his ships would be overwhelmed, but his troops would make the planet virtually unlivable, and he would kill more of the hated human enemy and their warships.

The ground battle continued on. Freed from orbital bombardment, Griswald ordered the two brigades of M1A1 battle tanks into combat. They engaged the Krieg armored personnel carriers and battle tanks. Armed with a 120mm cannon, the Abrams tanks could destroy an enemy vehicle at eight-thousand-two-hundred feet. Their sloped front armor could deflect the Keieg laser. However, the back and side armor were vulnerable to laser strikes.

The Krieg, not used to tank battles dispersed their armored vehicles. Observing the Krieg tactics, the senior brigade commander General Kidder employed blitzkrieg tactics with his spearhead punching through Krieg positions. There the turret-mounted machine guns could wreak havoc among the Kriegster soldiers behind their lines. It did not take long for the Krieg to discover and exploit the tank weakness, and their lasers began to knock out tanks.

The infantry exploited the tank breakthroughs in armored personnel carriers and MSARs. At close range, the hand-held railguns and M-16s engaged the Krieg and Kriegsters. With the arrival of the infantry, the Krieg could no longer focus on the tanks. Vicious close combat resulted. Casualties were heavy on both sides.

The Kriegster warriors finally located the dragon compound. As they massed to attack, Callahan ordered his reserved warbirds to begin dropping napalm bombs on the concentrations. The compound itself was defended by riders equipped with M-16's, handheld railguns and MSAR vehicles.

Several hundred of the Kreig and the Kriegsters attacked the compound secluded in the forest. The defenders beat back the first two attacks. The third attack advanced further but was decimated by the MSARs. The Kreig heavy weapons gouged out large sections of the compound walls. As the Kriegsters assaulted the breaches, they were repulsed by the MSAR teams. Finally, they broke through into the compound itself. The dragons swooped in ripping at the Kriegsters with their claws, injecting their poisons.

In the final melee, Emily was severely wounded by a Kriegster's energy weapon. Seeing her fall, the enraged dragons, heedless of their losses, tore into the remaining Kreig and Kriegsters ripping them apart until none were left.

Responding to urgent calls for assistance, the medical teams quickly arrived and administered emergency first aid to Emily and the other wounded defenders. Gravely wounded, Emily was placed on a stretcher, loaded into a medical evacuation helicopter and transported to the command center hospital. Hundreds of dragons and riders flew as escorts, swooping down to kill all the Kreig or Kriegsters they encountered on their journey.

Seeing dozens of dragons diving down on them, many of the Krieg dropped their weapons, and running on all fours tried to escape into the forests. The dragon's claws ripped them apart. Several of the Kriegsters tried to surrender. The vengeful dragons did not take any prisoners.

Chapter 38

Before the start final space battle of Delta Pavonis, Admiral Shepard addressed his warbird pilots and crew over intraship com. He advised them of the Krieg's new rail-gun point defense system. He commented that this Alpha male was more resourceful than the ones encountered in Andromeda, and adapted to the warbird threat.

Shepard advised them of the new attack strategy, and that the fleet warships would assist to burn holes into the point-defense screen. He finished wishing the pilots and crews good luck and good hunting.

Following the speech, the fleet began the launching of one-thousand warbirds including seven-hundred and fifty fighters and two-hundred and fifty bombers. The small craft orbited above the fleet.

The Krieg formation was as predicted by

Griswald. The cruiser and the two gunboats were in front as a shield, followed by the two battleships. Each of them was almost twice the size of the allied battlewagons.

The warbirds started to advance in three crescent-shaped waves. Colonels Burns, Quelly, Evans, and Major Fogtman led their squadrons into the battle. As they neared maximum railgun range, the allied battleships launched missiles and opened up with their laser which brightly illuminated the metallic wall created by the pellets. The battlewagons continued to fire to open up gaps. The warbirds also fired their laser to help clear a path in front of them.

Suddenly the warbirds encountered the metallic shield. Several of them disappeared from direct hits, and others spun out of control from hits on the wings and stabilizers. These pilots became easy targets for the point defense. The rest flew in with the crescent-shaped waves expanding to attack the Krieg warships from all sides.

The defensive fire was intense. Major Fogtman watched in dread as first Colonel Quelly's warbird, them Colonel Burn's winked off his screen. Mourning the potential loss of his friends, he pressed on with the attacks.

Within an hour, the initial phase was over. The one megaton hits from the fighters eventually took down the shield emitters. The next strikes opened up breaches in the picket ships' hulls. Then the bombers with their five megaton warheads finished the destruction.

The three Krieg picket ships exploded in nuclear fireballs. Over one hundred warbirds were destroyed or disabled. Dozens of pilots ejected, waiting for pick-up, or to freeze to death if the rescue shuttles were delayed.

Five hundred warbirds flew on against the battleships, while the others returned to their mother ships to be rearmed and refueled. The Krieg battleships fired their point defense railguns, resulting in an expanding wall of metal fragments similar to shotgun shells.

When the returning pilots were waiting for the installation of new weapons, they were debriefed about the missing pilots. Dozens of them identified pilots who ejected. Colonels Burns and Quelly were among those who bailed out into intense rail-gun fire.

The fleet's cruisers and frigates also closed on the Krieg battleships launching their missiles and shooting the lasers into the expanding layers of the railgun point defense. When the rockets struck the metal fragments, the multiple nuclear explosions burned holes in the metallic shield.

The allied warships conducted erratic maneuvers to avoid the counter fire from the Krieg laser batteries. However, two cruisers and three frigates exploded following several laser strikes which blew out their shield emitters, leaving them exposed to direct laser hits.

The warbirds swept past the allied ships, firing

their lasers into the expanding wall of metal fragments. Dozens of the pilots died as their planes were obliterated by the point defense. Dozens of others ejected into the maelstrom.

However, from all sides, the assault continued, with the nuclear warheads exploding near or against the Krieg shields. With hundreds of torpedoes and missiles approaching, the point defense could not shoot them all down. Numerous one megaton warheads detonated against the shields or onto the hull as the emitters overloaded dropping the shield strength. Torpedoes began to explode on or near the weakened battleship shields causing hull breaches and radioactive fallout inside the warships.

As the rearmed warbirds approached, the bombers went in launching their five-megaton warhead torpedoes against the mostly unprotected hulls of the Krieg battleships. The reduced point defense still shot down two dozen of the slower bombers, even as explosions erupted all along the length of the

Krieg warships.

The surviving bombers, after expending their loads broke off. The three hundred warbirds of the fourth wave attacked through greatly diminished point defense. One Torpedo after another detonated on or inside the battleships. Secondary explosions erupted, and the warships began to break apart like cracked eggs. The pilots broke off and escaped just as the reactor containment failed, and the Krieg battlewagons disappeared in nuclear fireballs.

The search and rescue shuttles retrieved fifty flight crews, many suffering severe injuries including radiation exposure.   Colonels Burns and Quelly were among the fortunate pilots rescued.   Both, protected by their escape capsules, sustained minor radiation exposure and were placed in decontamination units.

The butcher's bill of the victory came at a steep price. The crews of the two cruisers, the three frigates, and the flight crews of two hundred twenty warbirds were missing and presumed dead.

Chapter 39

Shepard's fleet turned around and returned to Delta Pavonis 4. He opened communications with General Griswald to determine the status of the ground battle.

Griswald replied, "Thank you for the timely relief. Your arrival turned the tide of the fight and deprived the Krieg of their orbital support. That allowed our warbirds and tanks to engage the enemy. Isolated pockets of the Krieg warriors are surrounded but are still fighting. There may be detachments of warriors in the forests or on the other continents. We will require your assistance in hunting them down.

"Our casualties were high. I am down to less than fifty percent effective soldiers. Fully one half of my tanks and warbirds were destroyed. Another half of those that remain are damaged. To my knowledge, all of the Krieg aircraft were shot down."

Then hesitating, Griswald asked, "Is the Secretary of Defense still with you?"

Robert Treat answered, "I am here. I offer you congratulations on your hard-fought victory. A grateful world appreciates you."

Griswald replied. "Can we talk privately?"

Shepard indicated that Robert could take the call in his ready room.

Robert picked up the phone and said with trepidation, "Is it, Emily? Is she still alive?"

Griswald answered, "Yes, but she is severely wounded. The doctors gave me bad news. The X-Rays indicate that she has cancer which has spread to multiple organs. She is not expected to survive more than a few weeks. Due to her condition, she is still in triage."

Somewhat relieved, Robert replied, "I am aware of her cancer, which is why I brought a team of Andromedan physicians to treat her.

"Please provide me with her position, and we will shuttle down."

Ten minutes later, Treat, the Andromedan physicians, their equipment, a stasis pod, and a security team departed *USSP Texas*. Five warbirds accompanied as escorts.

Robert and his team, pushing the wheeled stasis pod and the equipment resembling a carry-on suitcase, rushed to Emily's bed in the triage.

She was pale but conscious and smiled painfully when Robert held her hand and said,
"You came back for me. I knew you would. The silly doctors tell me it is too late to save me. I told them nonsense, I am not that easy to kill."

Robert smiled and said, "I am back and will never leave you again. My Andromedan friends will save you."

Brushing aside the hospital's medical staff, the Andromedan lead physician Androphosphene conducted their own body scans with hand-held equipment.   Gravely, he confirmed the diagnosis. Robert's heart sank. With tears forming in his eyes he whispered, "Isn't there anything you can do"?

Androphosphene opened the bag resembling a suitcase, scanned in his diagnostic findings and began entering data into the control panel of a black box with tubes extending from the bottom. Lights started flashing red, yellow, and green in sequence.   Androphosphene entered more data until all the lights turned green.

Smiling he said to Robert, "The diagnosis is correct, but their prognosis is wrong. I have prepared a solution of nanites which will most likely enable Emily to make a complete recovery. They will also be preventative for potential future medical issues."

The staff doctor asked,   "What are nanites, and what do they do"?

Androphosphene replied, "Nanites are microscopic, programmable organisms. Some of them will seek out and destroy the cancer cells. The others will heal the damage done by the energy weapon, and repair Emily's other organs which were on the verge of failure. When the nanites have done their assigned tasks, they will die and exit the body during normal excretion of waste."

He then connected the tube extensions into ports of the IV lines. Smiling confidently, Androphosphene continued, "Emily should be completely cured in sixty days. She will need to undergo additional nanite treatment for two days, then enter into stasis for transport back to Andromeda to continue the protocol.

"Nanite treatment is excruciatingly painful, and stasis is required to give her body time to heal. I will give her pain medication which will keep Emily comfortable until she enters the stasis pod. The nanites will continue their work for the duration of the voyage. More nanites will be administered when she reaches Andromeda." He then injected the pain medication into the IV lines.

Emily said to Robert, "You won't get rid of me easily and will keep me company in my dreams until I awake in your arms." She then sighed, blinked her eyes slowly, and dropped into a deep sleep.

Chapter 40

Mop-up activities on Delta Pavonis 4 lasted for one week. Shepard suggested that Griswald deploy the previously captured and deprogrammed Kriegsters and use them to broadcast to the Krieg-held pockets.

Following days of intense fighting, observing that they were abandoned by their fleet, and unwilling to follow their Krieg officers suicidal orders, the Kriegsters rebelled and executed their commanders. Then they offered to surrender. Following negotiations with their deprogrammed brethren, one-thousand Kriegsters laid down their weapons.

Utilizing procedures used in the previous deprogramming, the offending programmable implants were identified and surgically removed. The issue now presented was what to do with a new species of humans, almost evenly divided between male and female. They were not welcome in Andromeda, and the dragons would not tolerate their presence on Delta Pavonis. The temporary solution was to transfer them to the troop transports for resettlement on another planet.

Washington, DC

Admiral Shepard's allied fleet returned to Earth. In an international ceremony, the contributing nations received profound thanks, and the spacers were treated as heroes. Admiral Shepard was awarded a fifth star and became the Fleet Admiral of the United States Navy. President Bush personally decorated Robert Treat with the Medal of Freedom and provided a second medal for Emily in absentia.

The next day at the Cabinet meeting, Fleet Admiral Shepard was invited to attend. He and Robert Treat submitted their proposal for resettlement of the former Kriegsters to the uninhabited continent on Beta Hydri 4. There they could heal, prosper, and develop the resources of the area. Volunteer educators could set up schools to teach the Kriegsters about the United States Government, the Constitution, and how to self-govern themselves. The teachers could also train them to speak English, to better communicate with us. The military could also observe them and ensure they did not revert to the violent soldiers programmed by the Krieg. Eventually, they could be integrated into normal human society.

Following the limited debate, the cabinet unanimously approved the proposal. As Beta Hydri 4 was still under military jurisdiction, Congressional approval was not required. Vice President Davis suggested that Congress be allowed to vote on a non-binding resolution. In a voice vote, both the House and Senate approved.

One week later the troop ships entered orbit above Beta Hydri 4. The former Kriegsters bordered shuttles and transported down to the surface. Supply shuttles delivered sections for pre-fabricated housing. Construction crews carried heavy equipment down to assist in the construction of the settlement, which could be expanded to accommodate the anticipated arrival of their Andromedan brethren.

President Bush accepted Robert Treat's resignation as Secretary of Defense so he could travel to Andromeda to be there when Emily woke from her stasis treatment. Bush also provided Robert with the temporary position as ambassador to Andromeda, subject to confirmation by the Senate when he returned.

This appointment would grant Robert plenipotentiary status to negotiate treaties and trade agreements, subject to approval by the Senate. Robert thanked the President, then arranged for a shuttle to take him to the space station to begin his journey to a new life.

Chapter 41

One week after Robert's arrival, the doctors arranged to have Emily's stasis pod moved into a private bedroom. All the indicator lights still were green, and the room lighting was dimmed. Before awakening her, Androphosphene scanned Emily's body for any signs of cancer, and to ensure her organs were wholly healed. Smiling he said: "Open the pod and wake her up."

The medical technician pushed a few buttons, the lid irised open, and the sides silently lowered. The medical assistant placed a pressure injector to Emily's shoulder, injected her then stepped back. Emily slowly stirred, opened her eyes, looking around slightly disorientated. When she saw Robert at her side, her eyes lit up with pleasure. Realizing her nudity was covered by a sheet she said to Robert: "Either get me some clothes or both of us are going to embarrass everyone. It has been a long time."

Androphosphene smiled, pointed at the adjacent king size bed and said: "Robert, you can stay, the rest of us will leave."

As the door to the room closed. Robert brushed the sheet aside, easily lifted Emily out of the pod and carried her to the bed. The next two weeks were like a honeymoon with Robert and Emily visiting the scenic areas on Andromeda 4. Emily especially enjoyed the alpha sunrise as it rose above the giant gas giant Omegatron. The view was magnificent, illuminating Omegatron and its dozens of smaller satellites.

Robert then realized it was time to conduct himself as the ambassador. He visited with Minion and gained his approval to transfer the deprogrammed Kriegsters to Beta Hydri 4. He explained that the United States Government, which had dominion over the Beta Hydri system had approved the resettlement. Indeed, those Kriegsters who accompanied the Krieg to Delta Pavonis 4 were already building their settlement.

The next stop was Triberbrow where Robert and Emily met Commetrez. He also agreed in principle to an alliance, and to the transfer of the captive deprogrammed Kriegsters into Robert's custody.

With an auspicious new beginning, Robert and Emily returned to Andromeda 4 and chartered a passenger liner to transport the repatriated settlers to Beta Hydri 4. Minion provided the ship's captain with the previous smugglers' portal, which now was the principal route to Earth-controlled space.

After reaching orbit on Beta Hydri 4, Robert and Emily met with the military governor General Samuel Ortiz. They indicated they had two-thousand deprogrammed Kriegsters ready for settlement.

Ortiz corrected, "You mean Batamans. That is what the new settlers elected to call their sub-species of humanity. It was done in a popular election. They seem to enjoy their release from

Krieg slavery and appear genuinely appreciative of being offered the opportunity of acceptance and self-government. I am sure these additional settlers will receive a warm welcome."

After delivering the new settlers, Robert and Emily visited Delta Pavonis. Emily immediately traveled to the Dragon Center to meet with her children. The Dragons congregated around her as she fluffed their feathers and stroked their beaks. The new hatchlings, hesitant at first swarmed all around her, seeking Emily's attention. Eventually, Emily left the hatchery, refreshed by the dragons' reception.

Robert and Emily returned to Earth to a tumultuous ticker tape parade in New York City. President Bush invited them to a reception in the White House. Both of them testified before Congress, and the Senate unanimously approved Robert as the United States Ambassador to Andromeda.

A new era of cooperation between two

previously divergent species of humanity became a reality forged in blood and iron. The Andromedans provided scientific and medical advancements, and the Earthers provided the Andromedans with new energetic settlers for the devastated and depopulated former Krieg-ruled systems.

The Krieg and, their minions, were still out there, somewhere. The Andromedans constructed new hybrid battleship fleets to supplement their existing warships. Thousands of warbirds were rolling off the assembly lines. Flight schools were graduating thousands of pilots and flight crews. Optimism started to grow throughout humanity. Together, they were stronger.

Epilogue

The following month, Emily and Robert hosted a family reunion at the ambassador's residence on Andromeda 4. Emily felt complete surrounded by Robert IV, Ann, Abagail, her eight grandchildren, two sons-in-law, and a daughter-in-law. They all exclaimed how good she looked, particularly for a cancer survivor, and her recovery from severe wounds in the battle at the Dragon Center.

Emily smiled then said: "The Andromedan nanites are real miracle workers. Not only did they cure my cancer, and heal my wounds; but they also restored all my internal organs to normal function." Smiling brightly she revealed one of the reasons for the reunion.

"Your dad and I are having twins, a boy and a girl. We have named the boy William, after Robert's great grandfather, and the girl Aurora Dawn." Emily then passed around sonogram images showing two babies growing in her womb. Excitedly, Emily stated: "All the prenatal diagnostic testing indicates they are perfectly healthy and normal."

Emily then made her second announcement. "I resigned from my cabinet position. Doctor Androphosphene and I are setting up a new business opportunity here in Andromeda. It will be a rejuvenation clinic. The restoration of my ovaries and other internal organs demonstrated that customized nanite treatment to restore youthful vitality is an actual reality. Your Dad has several projects to wrap up. Then he is going to sleep for sixty days."

Afterward

This is the final chapter in the Manifest Destiny series. I hope you enjoyed reading this book and the series as much as I did as I created it.

Publicity on Amazon is generated by positive reviews. If you liked this book and the others in the series, please feel free to provide me with a review for each book.

I have selected a nexus point in Rome to twist for my next book. Let the fun continue.

Made in the USA
Monee, IL
29 September 2025

30991114R00184